ABOUT

Barbara Cartland, the novelist, who is also an political speaker and t written over 460 books and sold nearly 500 million copies all over the world.

She has also had many historical works published and has written four autobiographies as well as the biographies of her mother and that of her brother, Ronald Cartland, who was the first Member of Parliament to be killed in the last war. This book has a preface by Sir Winston Churchill and has just been republished with an introduction by the late Sir Arthur Bryant.

Love at the Helm a novel written with the help and inspiration of the late Earl Mountbatten of Burma, Great Uncle of His Royal Highness The Prince of Wales, is being sold for the Mountbatten Memorial Trust.

She has broken the world record for the last twelve years by writing an average of twenty-three books a year. In the Guinness Book of Records she is listed as the world's top-selling author.

Miss Cartland in 1978 sang an Album of Love Songs with the Royal Philharmonic orchestra.

In private life Barbara Cartland, who is a Dame of Grace of the Order of St John of Jerusalem, Chairman of the St John Council in Hertfordshire and Deputy President of the St John Ambulance Brigade, has fought for better conditions and salaries for Midwives and Nurses.

She championed the cause for the Elderly in 1956 invoking a Government Enquiry into the "Housing Conditions of Old People".

In 1962 she had the Law of England changed so that Local Authorities had to provide camps for their own Gypsies. This has meant that since then thousands and thousands of Gypsy children have been able to go to

School which they had never been able to do in the past, as their caravans were moved every twenty-four hours by the Police.

There are now fourteen camps in Hertfordshire and Barbara Cartland has her own Romany Gypsy Camp called Barbaraville by the Gypsies.

Her designs "Decorating with Love" are being sold all over the USA and the National Home Fashions League made her, in 1981, "Woman of Achievement".

Barbara Cartland's book, *Getting Older, Growing Younger* has been published in Great Britain and the USA and her fifth Cookery Book, *The Romance of Food*, is now being used by the House of Commons.

In 1984 she received at Kennedy Airport, America's Bishop Wright Air Industry Award for her contribution to the development of aviation. In 1931 she and two RAF Officers thought of, and carried the first aeroplane-towed glider air-mail.

During the War she was Chief Lady Welfare Officer in Bedfordshire looking after 20,000 Service men and women. She thought of having a pool of Wedding Dresses at the War Office so that a Service Bride could hire a gown for the day.

She bought 1,000 gowns without coupons for the ATS, the WAAFs and the WRNS. In 1945 Barbara Cartland received the Certificate of Merit from Eastern Command.

In 1964 Barbara Cartland founded the National Association for Health of which she is the President, as a front for all the Health Stores and for any product made as alternative medicine.

This has now a $500,000,000 turnover a year, with one third going in export.

In January 1988 she received "La Medaille de Vermeil de la Ville de Paris", (the Gold Medal of Paris). This is the highest award to be given by the City of Paris for ACHIEVEMENT – 25 million books sold in France.

In March 1988 Barbara Cartland was asked by the Indian Government to open their Health Resort outside Delhi. This is almost the largest Health Resort in the world.

Barbara Cartland was received with great enthusiasm by her fans, who also fêted her at a Reception in the city and she received the gift of an embossed plate from the Government.

by the same author in Pan

A Hazard of Hearts
The Temple of Love
A Revolution of Love
A Chieftain Finds Love
The Lovely Liar
The Passionate Princess
Revenge is Sweet
Solita and the Spies
A Knight in Paris
Paradise in Penang

BARBARA CARTLAND

LOVE AT FIRST SIGHT

Pan Original
Pan Books London, Sydney and Auckland

First published 1989 by Pan Books Ltd,
Cavaye Place, London SW10 9PG
9 8 7 6 5 4 3 2 1
© Cartland Promotions 1989
ISBN 0 330 30583 2
Phototypeset by Input Typesetting Ltd, London
Printed and bound in Great Britain by
Cox & Wyman Ltd, Reading

Author's Note

Arranged marriages for Royalty and the English aristocracy were continued until after World War I.

Queen Victoria arranged marriages for twenty-four of her relatives who married Royal Princes and Grand Dukes all over Europe.

In the reign of Edward VII there was no question of a Duke or Nobleman's daughter choosing her own husband.

Everything was arranged so that the girl was betrothed to the most important title and the bridegroom received with her either land or money.

It was only when Chaperons ceased to exist in 1918 that débutantes were allowed to go to Balls and parties with just a partner.

When I 'came out' in that year, my mother complained that there were no lobster suppers for Chaperons. In fact, they were not invited.

Most of the men who took me dancing had come out of the Services and were too poor to offer one anything but dancing after dinner in one of the smart Restaurants or Night Clubs.

It was then for the first time that girls could refuse to marry what previously had been the 'highest bidder', and could follow their hearts.

I had forty-nine proposals of marriage before I accepted the fiftieth!

Sociology:

You in the Home
The Fascinating Forties
Marriage for Moderns
Be Vivid, Be Vital
Love, Life and Sex
Vitamins for Vitality
Husbands and Wives
Men are Wonderful
Etiquette
The Many Facets of Love
Sex and the Teenager
The Book of Charm
Living Together
The Youth Secret
The Magic of Honey
The Book of Beauty and Health
Keep Young and Beautiful by Barbara Cartland and Elinor Glyn
Etiquette for Love and Romance
Barbara Cartland's Book of Health

Cookery:

Barbara Cartland's Health Food Cookery Book
Food for Love
Magic of Honey Cookbook
Recipes for Lovers
The Romance of Food

Editor of:

The Common Problem by Ronald Cartland (with a preface by the Rt.
Hon. the Earl of Selborne, P.C.)
Barbara Cartland's Library of Love
Barbara Cartland's Library of Ancient Wisdom
Written with Love Passionate love letters selected by Barbara Cartland

Drama:

Blood Money
French Dressing

Philosophy:

Touch the Stars

Radio Operetta:

The Rose and the Violet (Music by Mark Lubbock) Performed in 1942.

Radio Plays:

The Caged Bird: An episode in the life of Elizabeth Empress of Austria Performed in 1957.

General:

Barbara Cartland's Book of Useless Information with a Foreword by the Earl Mountbatten of Burma.
(In aid of the United World Colleges)
Love and Lovers (Picture Book)
The Light of Love (Prayer Book)
Barbara Cartland's Scrapbook
(In aid of the Royal Photographic Museum)
Romantic Royal Marriages
Barbara Cartland's Book of Celebrities
Getting Older, Growing Younger

Verse:

Lines on Life and Love

Music:

An Album of Love Songs sung with the Royal Philharmonic Orchestra.

Films:

The Flame is Love

Cartoons:

Barbara Cartland Romances (Book of Cartoons) has recently been published in the USA, Great Britain, and other parts of the world.

Children:

A Children's Pop-Up Book: *Princess to the Rescue*

Video:

A Hazard of Hearts

"LOVE AT FIRST SIGHT"
1880

Ila, whose real name is Lady Lavinia, is one of three sisters. Phyllis and Clementine's arranged marriages have both turned out unhappily.

Ila's father, the Duke of Cumberworth, tells her that their next-door neighbour, the Marquis of Rakemoore, wishes to marry her.

She learns it is to avoid being forced into marriage with one of Queen Victoria's less important German relatives.

Because Ila wants to marry for love she decides to run away.

As she escapes through a wood she sees coming towards her a little boy. He is riding a pony in the direction of a dangerous cliff.

Just in time she stops him although his pony falls into the ravine.

Ila is knocked unconscious and is carried to a house in the wood which, unbeknown to her, belongs to the Marquis of Rakemoore.

Then she realises that Robin, the boy she rescued, is his nephew.

Now she knows she will have to run away again.

How the Marquis finds her and falls in love without knowing who she is and how they eventually find happiness is told in this 439th book by Barbara Cartland.

Chapter One
1880

"God what a finish!"

The ejaculation came from the front of the Jockey Club Stand as the horses came down the straight.

Trumpeter, who belonged to the Marquis of Rakemoore, was the favourite.

The crowds were already beginning to chant, as they always did when the Marquis' horses were taking part on the racecourse, "Rake! Rake! Rake!"

Trumpeter was neck and neck with *Ladybird* who belonged to the Duke of Cumberworth.

Both owners were watching at the front of the Stand.

The Duke was flushed with excitement, his lips pressed together in an effort to prevent himself from shouting encouragement to his horse.

The Marquis on the other hand was, as usual, completely calm.

He had a cynical expression on his face which had become habitual.

Even his eyes did not seem to express any particular excitement.

At the same time, anyone who knew him very well would have been aware there was a little pulse beating in his neck.

It was the only thing about his body he could not control.

It was certainly an unexpectedly exciting race when

everybody had anticipated that *Trumpeter* would 'walk it'.

As it was, *Ladybird* had come up on the outside at the last moment and now the two horses were neck and neck.

As somebody said almost beneath his breath, "There is not a pin to put between them!" The noise from the crowd became deafening. Because the Marquis was an habitual winner, and certainly the most spectacular owner on the Turf, he had caught the public fancy.

They supported him uproariously, every time his horses won.

As this happened very frequently, it seemed as if he had grown used to their adulation.

He only smiled somewhat mockingly when they cheered him on and off the course.

It was of course the women who wished him 'Good Luck!' and thrust into his hand little bunches of white heather.

Whatever their age, women, young or old, pretty or plain, were captivated by the Marquis's appearance.

Over six feet tall with broad, square shoulders and the narrow hips of an athlete, he was exceedingly handsome.

It was only when he lost his boyish enthusiasm for life that the cynical lines appeared on his face.

There often seemed to be a somewhat sarcastic note in his voice when he was talking to some beautiful woman.

He had begun to look like his name – Rake. It was what he was called by even his closest friends.

But only now did it seem really applicable. At the same time he did not really desire to be raffish.

It was something which had happened! His name, tradition and his environment all had something to do with it.

"The trouble with you, Rake," one of his friends said to him, "is that you have too much, and too little competition."

16

"I don't know what you mean by that," the Marquis replied.

In actual fact he was well aware that the latter part of the sentence was true.

He had achieved everything far too easily. He had not been given a challenge which, when he thought about it, was essential for a man of his age.

Now at nearly thirty, he was beginning to think he had tasted all the delights that were to be had in the Social World in which he moved.

The same applied to the Sporting World in which he reigned supreme.

Last year, his horses had won the Grand National at Aintree and the Gold Cup at Ascot.

They had also been an easy first in a number of other Classic Races.

"There really is not much point in us competing against you, Rakemoore!" one of the members of the Jockey Club remarked. "In fact, as far as I am concerned, race meetings are becoming just a One-Man-Horse-Show!"

He was particularly piqued because his horse had not been in the first three.

The Marquis did not bother to reply.

Yet when he returned home, he wondered if there was not some truth in what had been said.

Did his horses and his Jockeys really need more competition?

Now, unexpectedly, in the big race at Epsom, his chief Jockey on *Trumpeter* was having to exert himself considerably more than he had expected.

The winning-post was just ahead.

The Marquis could see his Jockey's whole body straining with the effort of pushing *Trumpeter* ahead of *Ladybird*.

The roar of the crowd grew louder.

Then, as the two horses passed the white post, the Duke gave an exclamation that was almost a cry:

"A dead heat, dammit!"

"I think you are right," the Marquis said in a slow, controlled voice.

For a moment the Duke was incapable of answering him.

Then, because he too was a sportsman, he said:

"Well, I certainly gave you a run for your money, Rakemoore!"

"It was one of the best races I have watched for a long time!" the Marquis replied.

"I have just thought," the Duke said, "as *Ladybird's* Dam is outstanding, if she was served by your stallion, we might breed the champion of all time."

The Marquis smiled.

"It is certainly an idea!"

"It seems quite a sensible one," the Duke remarked, "considering our estates march with each other's. And I have another proposition to put to you."

"What is that?" the Marquis asked.

Both the owners were talking as they moved out of the Stand, knowing they had to watch their Jockeys being weighed in.

"My third daughter is unmarried," the Duke replied, "and I think, if nothing else, you would have a bond in your knowledge of horseflesh."

He laughed as if he had made a joke, but the Marquis stiffened.

His lips set in a hard line.

He moved quickly ahead so that there was no possibility of his replying to the Duke's suggestion.

He walked towards the paddock.

He was thinking as he did so that this was typical of the Duke of Cumberworth!

Only he would suggest he should marry his daughter at

a moment when they were both concerned with a very outstanding race.

"Why the devil cannot people leave me alone?" the Marquis asked himself.

At the same time, he automatically raised his hat to a very attractive woman.

She reached out to put her gloved hand on his arm.

"Congratulations, Rake!" she said in a soft, seductive voice. "I knew you would win."

"I suppose half a loaf is better than no bread!" the Marquis replied, and passed on.

There was a number of other women to clutch at his arm.

Or else they looked up at him, an invitation in their eyes and a provocative pout to their lips.

By the time he reached his horse the Marquis had raised his hat a dozen times.

He had been congratulated by too many people for him to count them.

Now, as he patted *Trumpeter's* neck, his Jockey said:

"I did me best, M'Lord, but I ain't never 'eard o' that *Ladybird* afore!"

"You have heard of her now!" the Marquis retorted, "and we shall doubtless hear a great deal more in the future."

He was appraising the Duke's mare as he spoke.

He told himself he had been very obtuse in not realising before the race that she was outstanding.

The Duke was certainly delighted with his horse, his Jockey and himself.

He accepted the congratulations of his friends, beaming on them almost as if he personally had been riding *Ladybird*.

The Marquis knew better than anyone that it was a great achievement to have nearly beaten *Trumpeter*.

He could not help thinking that his stable had for once come up against some really stiff competition.

"They had begun to take things too easy." he reprimanded himself.

He knew in a way it was his own fault.

The members of the Jockey Club were clustering round the Duke.

It was obvious that they thought it was an achievement that had been needed for some time.

Having watched his Jockey weigh in, the Marquis walked slowly back to the Paddock.

He had a horse entered for the next race, but he had no chance of winning. Because the horse had never run in a big race before, he was trying it out.

It was being ridden by a young Jockey to whom he was also giving a chance to show his paces.

He might be an asset in the future, or he might not.

At the moment, like the horse, he was an 'unknown quantity'.

Then when the Marquis saw the other horses entered for the race he told himself it was a waste of time to stay and watch it.

His Manager was present at the meeting.

He would give him an account of how his horse had fared and if the Jockey was worth retaining.

He therefore decided to return to London.

He did not stop to say goodbye to anybody but simply walked to where his Phaeton was waiting.

He climbed into the driving seat.

It bored him to be long on the roads, especially when the traffic was heavy.

His Phaeton therefore was drawn by a team of his fastest horses, all jet-black.

They complemented his Phaeton which was black with yellow wheels and upholstery.

These were the Marquis' racing colours and were as noticeable as he was himself.

As he drove towards the gate, the men in the crowd waved their hats, the ladies their handkerchiefs.

There was a cry of:

"Rake! Rake! Good Luck! God bless you!"

This was taken up by the crowds outside the Racecourse.

Drivers of vehicles on the road good-humouredly moved to make way for him as if it was his right.

Because the Marquis had left early, once he was away from the vicinity of the racecourse, the traffic thinned out.

His horses were then able to carry him as swiftly as he wished them to.

He was thinking as he went.

He decided he would make it perfectly clear to his Manager, his grooms and his Jockeys that they must 'pull up their socks'.

He was determined the same sort of thing would not happen on any other occasion.

He could not remember when, in a big race, his horse had not been first past the winning-post.

There had certainly never been a dead heat before.

The Marquis reached London, as he expected, in record time.

He drew up with a flourish outside his house in Park Lane.

As he did so he was surprised to see a chaise drawn by one horse waiting outside.

He was almost certain that he had no engagements until the evening.

Then he was dining with Lady Wisbourne, which was something to which he was looking forward.

Muriel Wisbourne was one of the outstanding Beauties.

It was inevitable that she and the Marquis should become attracted to each other.

The Marquis would have been mock-modest if he had not realised that, together, they might have stepped down from Olympus.

Even the most blasé people drew in their breath when they saw them together.

Lady Wisbourne was just another in a long line of Beauties with whom the Marquis had been associated.

He kept the gossips shaking their heads and whispering about him from dusk until dawn.

Two grooms who had been awaiting his arrival went to the horses' heads.

The Marquis stepped down from his Phaeton to walk up the red carpet and into the hall.

There were four footmen on duty.

The Butler, a pontifical figure with white hair, came forward to say:

"I trust Your Lordship had a good day?"

"Very good!" the Marquis replied briefly. "Who is here?"

"Captain Brentwood, M'Lord."

The Marquis was relieved.

For a moment he had thought it might be some bore who wished to talk to him.

It would be about either a Charity in which he was not interested or some young relative who wanted employment.

This was an habitual occurrence as the Marquis had such a wide variety of interests.

He had become, he said jokingly, a 'Labour Bureau' for almost every man he met.

There were youths he was quite certain would be hopeless as Farm Managers or in any sort of executive post.

The older men had either returned from a well-known Regiment, or had fallen on hard times.

They thought that, with his very wide interests, there must be room for them.

And of course, they all required large salaries which they could not obtain elsewhere.

Having handed his hat and riding gloves to a footman, the Marquis followed his Butler to the Study.

The door was opened for him.

He found his friend Peregrine Brentwood sitting comfortably in an armchair with a glass of champagne in his hand.

"Hello, Perry!" the Marquis said. "I was not expecting you!"

"You are early," Peregrine Brentwood remarked, "but I suppose you won?"

"A dead heat with Cumberworth's mare!"

"I do not believe it!" Peregrine exclaimed. "The betting in White's Club was so 'Odds-on' that I did not bother to put down my money!"

"You were quite right," the Marquis said, "and I must say, Cumberworth's horse *Ladybird* is outstanding. I should have realised it before the race started."

Peregrine Brentwood laughed.

"It is unlike you to be caught napping!"

"That is what I thought myself," the Marquis said with a wry smile.

He helped himself to a glass of champagne from the bottle that stood in a silver ice bucket on the grog-table.

As he walked to stand in front of the fireplace he asked:

"Have you come to see me about anything in particular?"

"You are thought-reading, as you always do!" Peregrine replied. "And the answer is 'yes'!"

The Marquis sat down and asked in a different tone of voice:

"What has happened?"

"I have something to tell you which I am afraid will upset you," Peregrine replied.

"Upset me?" the Marquis asked curiously.

It flashed through his mind that Lord Wisbourne had turned nasty over his association with his wife.

It would not be a surprise if he had.

The Marquis was well known to be a menace to any beautiful woman.

Jealous husbands were reputed to hurry their pretty wives to the country if he so much as looked in their direction.

It was said that quite a number of them regretted the passing of the chastity belt.

Although it was against the Law and certainly against the wishes of Queen Victoria, duels did take place.

The Marquis had been involved in two, both of which most unfairly had left him the victor.

He had emerged without a scratch.

His opponents, who had every reason to call him out, had their arms in slings for nearly a month.

Lord Wisbourne was an older man.

The Marquis thought it very unlikely that he would risk the scandal of a duel.

But of course, one could never be certain how far a man would go when he thought his honour was at stake.

Peregrine was being unaccountably silent and the Marquis said:

"Well? Out with it! I might as well know the worst."

Peregrine put down his glass of champagne.

"You know, Rake," he said, "that my Uncle is the Lord Chamberlain?"

"Yes, of course," the Marquis replied.

He wondered as he spoke how this could possibly have anything to do with him.

"I am very fond of him," Peregrine went on, "and after

my parents died I more or less made my home with him and his charming wife."

The Marquis thought he must have been aware of all this.

But as Peregrine was in the Household Brigade he was housed in the Barracks.

He had not therefore connected him very closely in his mind with Windsor Castle.

"Last night," Peregrine continued, "because I had no invitations which interested me and you were with Muriel Wisbourne, I dined with my Uncle who was also alone."

The Marquis wondered where all this was leading.

"Afer dinner," Peregrine said, "Uncle Lionel told me that the Queen is sending for you today. She would have done so yesterday, but she remembered you would be at the Races."

"The Queen is sending for me?" the Marquis asked. "What for?"

Peregrine looked at him as he said slowly:

'The Princess Greta of Saxe-Coburg is arriving in England at the end of the week!"

The Marquis stared at his friend.

"What has that to do with me?"

Peregrine did not reply and after a minute the Marquis said incredulously:

"You cannot mean . . . it is – impossible!"

"She is a distant Cousin of the late-lamented Prince Consort," Peregrine said, "and the Queen is anxious that she should be married to somebody suitable."

"Suitable!" the Marquis exclaimed. "I am damned if I will marry some dreary German *Frau* to please the Queen or anybody else!"

"I told my Uncle that you have no intention of marrying," Peregrine replied.

"What did he say to that?" the Marquis enquired.

"He said Her Majesty has thought for some time that

you needed a wife. The actual expression was to 'steady you down'."

"My God! I have never heard of such a thing!" the Marquis exploded.

He knew as he spoke that it was exactly what he might have expected from the Queen.

She had been busy marrying off her own relatives and doing her best for Prince Albert's ever since he died.

The Marquis was well aware that he would not have been allowed to marry anyone who was an important Royal.

But the Saxe-Coburgs were a very large family.

They had not been of any importance until Prince Albert became the Consort of the Queen of England.

He could imagine nothing more ghastly than finding himself 'lumbered' with a German girl with whom he would have nothing in common.

If he was truthful, he did not like the Germans.

Those he had met to date he had found singularly lacking in any sense of humour.

"I am sorry, Rake," Peregrine was saying. "I knew it would upset you, but I thought it was only right that I should tell you before you went blithely to Windsor Castle."

"If you think I am going there to let the Queen order my private life about and tell me whom I should marry, you are very much mistaken!" the Marquis said sharply.

"I told my Uncle that would be your attitude," Peregrine replied, "and he said that actually, you have no choice. The invitation will be a Royal Command!"

The Marquis rose and walked to the grog-table to fill up his glass with champagne.

It was very unusual for him to drink more than one glass at this hour of the day.

He was, in fact, extremely abstemious when it came to wine and rich food.

Now he felt as if he had been confronted suddenly by a maelstrom and had no idea what he could do about it.

He now remembered what he had almost forgotten that the Queen was his Godmother.

The Marchioness of Rakemoore was traditionally a Lady of the Bed Chamber.

When he had been christened it had been a great honour that Her Majesty had signified her willingness to be a Godparent.

Now, he thought bitterly, she doubtless thought she was doing him another favour.

"I am sorry, Rake," Peregrine said again.

"There must be some way out of this," the Marquis answered. "For God's sake, Perry, tell me what I can do!"

"I have been thinking about it all day," Peregrine replied.

"Have you seen the woman?" the Marquis enquired.

"No," Peregrine answered, "but I have seen her sister who was married to a Frenchman, the Comte of something or other. I met them both at the French Embassy last year."

"And what was she like?" the Marquis asked.

"Just what you might expect – big, fat, with nothing to say and, when she did speak, very guttural."

The Marquis walked across the room to the window and back again.

"I will not do it!" he said. "I will go abroad rather than be tied to a woman I would want to murder a few hours after she had become my wife!"

As he spoke he thought of the perfection of his houses, especially Rake, his ancestral home.

It was undisputably one of the most beautiful houses in England.

Having been added to all down the centuries, its contents were the envy of every connoisseur.

The Marquis was exceedingly proud of his ancestors.

One of the most distinguished of them had served Queen Elizabeth.

But the one who had been most remarkable had been an adviser to King Charles II.

The story was told and retold so that every member of the family believed it to be true.

A Moore, which was the family name, had been a Rake like his King, and the two of them had become close friends.

A dinner party had been given just after Christmas in the Palace of Whitehall.

The beautiful Barbara Castlemaine had asked King Charles if he had made a resolution for the New Year.

He smiled and replied gallantly:

"What could it be, Barbara, but to make love to you more ardently than I have done so far!"

The Courtiers sitting round the table had all laughed.

The King, turning to his friend Moore, asked him:

"What is yours? And do not tell me it is the same as mine, or I shall have you beheaded!"

Moore's eyes had twinkled.

"My wish, Sire, is that I should be more of a Rake than I am at the moment."

The King had thrown back his head and laughed.

Then he exclaimed.

"That is what I have been seeking – a good name for you! 'Rakemoore' and you shall be the first Earl with that name!"

From then on it had been a tradition that the head of the family – who a hundred years later had risen to be a Marquis – should be a 'Rake'.

In fact, it would have been a disappointment if he had been anything else.

Now, out of the blue, the Queen had decided that enough was enough.

28

The Marquis knew it was because Lady Wisbourne was one of her hereditary Ladies-in-Waiting.

Before her there had been another beautiful Peeress with whom he had had a fiery and somewhat indiscreet *affaire de coeur*.

"Help me, Perry," the Marquis said now. "There must be some way out of this! Would it be any use talking to your Uncle?"

Peregrine shook his head.

"I asked Uncle Lionel the same thing, and because he admires you as a sportsman – and who does not? – I think he is sorry that you are to be leg-shackled to a German."

Peregrine's voice deepened as he said:

"My Uncle's actual words were: 'The only possible excuse the Marquis could give for refusing to accede to the Queen's command would be if he were either married or engaged to be married to somebody else.'"

For a moment there was silence.

Then the Marquis remembered what the Duke had said to him when they were together in the Jockey Club Stand.

It was almost like a light in the darkness.

God knows, he had no wish to marry anyone!

It was a question of a fat German with whom he had nothing in common, or an English girl!

As the Duke had said, at least his daughter and he both would have an interest in horses.

"I will do it!" he said aloud.

"Do what?" Peregrine enquired.

"Marry the Duke of Cumberworth's daughter!"

Peregrine stared at him.

"What are you talking about?"

"The Duke suggested today after our horses passed the winning-post together that we could breed an exceptional animal out of *Ladybird's* Dam and *Trumpeter*."

"That is certainly a good idea!" Peregrine exclaimed.

The Marquis ignored the interruption and went on:

"He also said, which I thought was damned impertinent at the time, that as our estates marched with each other's, I might marry his third daughter, and at least we would share an interest in horses."

"I had forgotten there was a third," Peregrine remarked. "If she is anything like the other two, she will be pretty; and she is English.'

"That is what I am thinking," the Marquis agreed.

"If you are serious, then you will have to hurry," Peregrine said. "I expect you will get your orders tonight. In fact, for all we know, they might be here now."

"I will find out," the Marquis said. "And if this is all a lot of nonsense, and you have got me worked up for nothing, I will wring your neck!"

"I promise you one thing," Peregrine replied, "I would not have upset you, if I had not known it was serious!"

The Marquis did not answer.

He was waiting for the door to open.

Then, as the Butler stood there, he asked:

"Is there a message for me from Buckingham Palace?"

"A letter was delivered just now, M'Lord, after you returned. I was waiting for the first opportunity to bring it to Your Lordship's notice."

As the Butler spoke he brought, as if by magic, a gold salver from behind his back.

On it was a large envelope which both the Marquis and Peregrine knew came from the Lord Chamberlain's Office.

The Marquis took it from the salver and the Butler withdrew.

He read his name on the front of the envelope, then flung the letter into Peregrine's lap.

"You open it," he said. "I know what it contains, and it merely makes me want to swear!"

Peregrine did as he was told, raising the flap of the envelope which was not very well stuck down.

He read the letter, then said:

"It is what we expected. Her Majesty wishes to see you at Windsor at 2.30 p.m. tomorrow afternoon."

The Marquis made no comment.

He merely walked to the window to look out with unseeing eyes at the garden which lay at the back of the house.

It was bright with Spring flowers and the trees with their green leaves were a picture in themselves.

Instead, he was seeing the long Dining-Room at Rake where he had given so many amusing parties.

He had always accepted the fact that one day he must produce an heir to the Marquisate.

This meant he would have to take a wife.

He tried to imagine her at the end of the table opposite him wearing the Rakemoore jewels which were unique.

She would look like his mother when she had sat there.

He had always thought that the woman who took his mother's place would be beautiful.

But she would also have the same sort of character and personality.

His mother had died when he was only ten.

The Marquis could never forget how gentle, gracious and dignified she had been.

When she had come to his room to say goodnight to him before she went down to dinner, she had always held him close in her arms.

He could still recall the scent of violets.

She had heard his prayers.

Then, after she had kissed him good-night, she would say:

"God keep you, my darling, and the angels watch over you while you sleep."

When she had died there had been a great void in his life.

It was something the Marquis had tried to forget because it hurt him so unbearably to think of it.

He missed her, he wanted her and he needed her.

Then, inevitably, because in the next few years he had grown so handsome, there were the women who fawned.

They said flattering things to him.

Even before he left Eton they were falling into his arms.

It would have been impossible, he knew, to refuse anything so tempting.

It was so easy in that he did not even have to raise a finger to attract them.

He had never thought of any of the women to whom he made love as being in any way comparable to his mother.

Nor did they touch the place she still held in his heart.

Now, without being able to choose for himself, he would be compelled to take a wife he had not even seen.

Or else be forced into marriage with a German because it was the Queen's wish.

After telling him what was written in the letter, Peregrine had remained silent.

The Marquis did not speak for some long time.

Then at last he turned from the window.

"Very well," he said and his voice was hard and sharp. "I will write to the Duke saying that I have considered his suggestion and will call on him at eleven o' clock tomorrow morning to discuss it further."

Peregrine was silent for a moment. Then he said:

"I suppose Cumberworth is in London?"

The Marquis, who had sat down again at his desk, looked at his friend in surprise.

"You mean he may have gone to the country?"

"I should have thought it more likely," Peregrine said. "It is where he stays the majority of his time."

"I had not thought of that."

The Marquis pondered for a moment. Then he said:

"I will leave at once for Rake – I shall have to cancel my evening with Muriel Wisbourne – and you had better come with me, otherwise I shall undoubtedly throw myself into the lake!"

Peregrine laughed.

"If you are thinking of drowning, that would be impossible, considering how well you swim! Cheer up Rake, it might not be as bad as you think."

"It might easily be worse!" the Marquis retorted.

Peregrine rose to his feet saying:

"If you wish to get to Rake in time for dinner we will have to leave at once. You can see the Duke after breakfast, then be on your way to London."

"You are making it sound like the Grand Tour!" the Marquis complained.

"I am sorry for you, Rake, I am, really!" Peregrine answered. "But I assure you, the Duke's daughter really is the best of two evils!"

"That is the right word," the Marquis said bitterly. "An evil which will make me loathe my Bride from the moment I put the ring on her finger!"

Chapter Two

Driving with a speed which only he could achieve, the Marquis and Peregrine reached Rake just after eight o' clock.

The Marquis was of course driving a different team from the one he had used going to the Races.

They were, however, as fast, if not faster.

Watching him, Peregrine thought there was no one who could drive better.

If he had lived in the Regency era, he would certainly have been acclaimed a Corinthian.

They did not talk as the Marquis had to concentrate on his horses.

He was also quite obviously both angry and depressed.

When they went down the long drive with his house ahead of them, Peregrine exclaimed:

"One thing is certain, Rake, you have not lost your touch when it comes to horseflesh!"

As he spoke he thought he had not been very tactful.

He was implying that the Marquis had not been so successful over his bride.

He glossed over his remark by making a joke which made the Marquis laugh.

The Butler was waiting for them at the top of the steps.

Two footmen rolled down the red carpet.

Rake was a magnificent house. In fact everybody who

saw it thought it was one of the most beautiful they had ever seen.

The Marquis' great-grandfather had commissioned the Adams brothers in the middle of the eighteenth century to improve it.

They had put a façade on what had been a jumble of architecture added to down the centuries.

The result was enormous but at the same time amazingly spectacular.

There were urns and statues on the roof, as well as the Marquis' Standard.

The long flight of steps leading up to the Ionic columns might have been brought from a Temple in Greece.

Every time he came to Rake Peregrine thought it was a house out of every man's dreams.

He was aware that the Marquis had been struck a body-blow.

The Marquis was, at that moment, gloomily contemplating his future.

Even the beauty of his house could not cheer him up.

There were baths waiting for both men in their bedrooms.

When they came downstairs twenty minutes later in their evening clothes, Peregrine thought the Marquis looked more overwhelmingly omnipotent than usual.

They talked sport all through the dinner which was excellent.

Only when they moved into the Marquis' Library, where he habitually sat when he was alone, did he say:

"I suppose I shall not have to rush into the marriage ceremony, even if the engagement is announced."

Peregrine knew he had been turning it over in his mind, and he replied:

"I imagine the Duke will want the marriage to take place before the end of the Season."

The Marquis's lips tightened.

He knew that meant the beginning of July at the very latest.

He was actually thinking that perhaps, if he was clever, he might persuade his fiancée that they were unsuited to each other.

Therefore they could announce that the marriage would not take place.

Yet he had the uncomfortable feeling that any woman, without exception, would be proud to bear his title.

Also the Duke would be so pleased at having him for a son-in-law that he would think the quicker they were married the better.

Because there was really nothing to talk about, the two men went to bed early.

The Marquis spent a restless night thinking that his days of freedom were numbered.

"I have been caught, captured and enslaved!" he told himself bitterly.

He slept a little before dawn but was up before he was called.

He dressed himself with a skill which always annoyed his valet.

He had practically finished his breakfast when Peregrine came into the room.

They had arranged last night that Peregrine would return to London alone.

The Marquis would go to Windsor straight after seeing the Duke.

His Secretary, to whom he had spoken before he returned, had already arranged that there would be a change of horses waiting for him at the Castle.

Then after he had seen the Queen, he would return to London as quickly as possible.

The Marquis had horses at posts on most of the main roads.

His organisation was so good that he seldom had to travel with horses that were tired.

"What are you doing this evening?" Peregrine asked as the Marquis finished his breakfast.

"I am going to see Muriel Wisbourne, if she is free tonight," the Marquis answered, "and I suppose that is something I shall not be able to do for very much longer."

He spoke bitterly, and Peregrine replied:

"It is no use kicking against the pricks, Rake. With your intelligence you ought to be able to make the best of them."

"How?" the Marquis asked harshly.

"Perhaps the girl will turn out to be better than you expect. If she is young and perhaps intelligent, you will be able to teach her how to do exactly what you want."

"From all I have seen of young girls, they are either gauche and shy, or else they giggle!" the Marquis said.

Peregrine laughed. Than he answered:

"Do not forget that Muriel Wisbourne and all the other Beauties like her were débutantes once and although you would not have given them a second glance, some man taught them to be as they are now!"

"I suppose that is true," the Marquis agreed, as if he had not thought of it.

"What you have to convince yourself," Peregrine went on, "is that your Bride, however 'raw' and inexperienced she may seem at the moment, will after a few years, be graceful, witty and sophisticated."

He paused a moment and then went on:

"Besides she will undoubtedly be looking for a Rake like yourself to flirt with!"

It flashed through the Marquis' mind that the last thing he wanted was a wife who would behave like Muriel Wisbourne.

Nor for that matter like any of the other Beauties with whom he had been associated.

He had always felt it was somehow embarrassing to eat another man's food, drink his wine, then seduce his wife.

It was, however, acceptable behaviour in Mayfair.

The pace had been set by the Prince of Wales and the Marquis had come to think of it as part of his everyday life.

Now he wondered if the future would really mean that he had to teach his wife to behave like the women who had been his mistresses.

The idea actually shocked him.

Because he had no wish to discuss it with Peregrine, he rose to his feet saying:

"I had better be on my way. I have sent a groom to tell the Duke to expect me, so he will doubtless have both his mares and his daughter on Parade!"

Peregrine laughed.

"I wonder which he will show you first?" he questioned.

The Marquis did not reply. He merely said:

"Goodbye, Perry. If I get away from the Duke in time, I will drop into White's Club to see if you are there."

"I shall naturally want to know what has happened," Peregrine said.

The Marquis paused for a moment.

"I suppose I ought to thank you for having saved me from being 'caught in the Royal trap'."

"It is my good deed for at least a year!" Peregrine laughed.

He had followed the Marquis from the Breakfast-Room and now they were in the hall.

The Butler was waiting for them.

"I think, M'Lord," he said to the Marquis, "Mr Barrett wishes to speak to Your Lordship about Master Robin."

"Master Robin?" the Marquis exclaimed. "What has he been up to now?"

"Mr Barrett wishes to discuss that with Your Lordship."

"I have not the time now," the Marquis answered. "I will come back the day after tomorrow and he can tell me then."

"Very good, Your Lordship."

The Marquis hurried down the steps and stepped into a very smart Curricle.

It was drawn by yet another team of exceptionally fine bays.

Peregrine looked at them with admiration.

"Goodbye Rake," he said waving his hand, but the Marquis made no reply.

There was a scowl between his eyes as he drove off, a groom sitting up behind him with crossed arms.

Peregrine turned to walk back into the house.

Bates, the Butler, followed him.

"I didn't realise," he said as if he were speaking to himself, "that His Lordship wouldn't be returning here today, an' Mr Barrett was very anxious to see him."

"What has that small boy been up to now?" Peregrine asked.

Bates sighed.

"There's nothing we can do wi' him, Sir," he said. "Nothing, an' that's th' truth!"

The Marquis was thinking the same thing as he drove down the drive.

He had deliberately not asked about his nephew last night.

He knew anything he heard would be bad news and he thought he had endured enough of that already.

Robin Moore, aged seven, was the son of his only brother who had been killed in a hunting accident eighteen months ago.

The Marquis had been very fond of his brother and was deeply upset at the time.

He had done his best to look after his brother's widow and her son.

Unfortunately Lady Guy Moore had always been a fragile creature.

The shock of the death of her husband, whom she adored, had proved too much for her.

She had slipped into a decline and died six months ago.

The Marquis found himself the Guardian of his nephew Robin.

He thought that various of his relations would be only too pleased to give the boy a home if he paid them for doing so.

Unfortunately Robin had proved to be an aggressive, almost uncontrollable child.

Within a month of being with the relatives the Marquis had chosen for him, he had been returned to Rake.

The Marquis had then provided him with a Governess, but she too had found him impossible.

Robin had several other Governesses, all of whom had left for the same reason – he was impossible.

The Marquis was certain now that the reason why Mr Barrett wished to speak to him was to tell him that yet another Governess had left.

The last one, he had been told, had left saying that Robin was the 'Spawn of Satan'.

She would, she declared, no longer stay at Rake, even if she were paid a million pounds a year for doing so!

"What am I to do with the boy?" the Marquis asked himself.

He was too young to send to School and the Marquis supposed he would have to find him a Tutor.

A man would deal with him physically as well as mentally.

There was one thing the Marquis had learned from his own experience.

40

It was that beating a child only made him more obstinate and aggressive than he was already.

Yet it was quite obvious: Robin could not be argued into behaving better.

The Governesses had made it clear that he made no response except rudeness.

The only thing in his favour was that Robin was an excellent rider.

It would have been surprising if he were not, seeing that his father had been nearly as good as the Marquis.

He had ridden since he was old enough to stay in the saddle.

The only time he behaved himself more or less like an ordinary human being was when he was on a horse.

But even then, he would not obey anybody.

The Marquis had given orders that he was to be accompanied at all times by two grooms.

He hoped that one of them, at any rate, would be able to keep the child under control.

He had a feeling, however, that this would be as hopeless as everything else had been.

As he drove across the boundary of his land into the Duke's he wondered if his future wife would be able to cope with Robin.

Then he remembered that the woman he was to marry was little more than a child herself.

He knew that she was likely to be as much of a problem as his nephew.

"Why the hell has this happened to me?" he asked himself.

It was the cry men had made since the beginning of time, when they were up against an obstacle that was too big to jump.

It took him only a half an hour to reach the Duke's house.

It was longer by road than it was across country.

Compared to Rake, Worth Castle was disappointing.

It was large, unwieldy and had no particular architectural beauty about it.

It was, however, situated in picturesque gardens with a protective wood at the back of it.

The Marquis was not at this moment concerned with the Duke's house.

He realised, however, he had not seen it for a long time.

He remembered now that the Duchess had died a year ago.

As the Cumberworths were so much older than he was, they had not been included in his parties.

In fact, he only saw the Duke at Race Meetings, or occasionally at some County gathering.

He thought with no pleasure that he would undoubtedly see a great deal more of him in the future.

Because he was expected, the Butler was waiting at the front door.

He was taken straight to the Duke's Study where His Grace was waiting to greet him.

He rose from the desk at which he was sitting to hold out his hand.

"This is certainly a surprise, Rakemoore!" he remarked. "When we met yesterday at the races, I had no idea you intended returning to the country."

"I did not know myself," the Marquis answered.

The Duke indicated an armchair in front of the fireplace.

"I suppose it's too early to offer you a drink?" he suggested.

"I have just had breakfast," the Marquis replied, "and I cannot stay long as I am on my way to Windsor."

"Ah – now I understand!" the Duke said. "You want to talk to me about my mares, and I want to show them to you. They are outstanding, if I do say so."

"You certainly proved that yesterday with *Ladybird*," the Marquis agreed.

The Duke's eyes seemed to light up.

"Gave you a bit of a surprise, did I not? It was what I hoped I would do."

"And you succeeded!" the Marquis admitted.

"When can I expect your stallion?" the Duke asked.

"There is something else I wish to speak to you about," the Marquis said.

The Duke looked surprised and he continued:

"It is in fact about the other suggestion you made as we left the Stand."

The Duke thought for a moment. Then he exclaimed:

"Are you saying – Well, of course you are – that you are interested in Lavinia!"

"You did mention that you had a third unmarried daughter," the Marquis said.

"Yes, yes, of course, of course!" the Duke said. "Lavinia is eighteen, and at the end of this month she will be out of mourning for her mother. She will of course, be presented at Court, and I want to see her happily married."

The Marquis drew in his breath.

"I am asking your permission to pay my addresses to Lady Lavinia."

It was with a superhuman effort that he managed to force the words from between his lips.

"My dear young man, nothing would give me greater pleasure than to welcome you as my son-in-law!" the Duke replied.

He got to his feet obviously delighted as he had been the previous day when his horse had won the race with *Trumpeter*.

He went to the side of the fireplace and seized the bell pull.

The door opened almost immediately and he said to the Butler:

"Bring a bottle of champagne as quickly as possible!"

"Very good, Your Grace."

When the door was shut behind him the Duke said;

"My luck is obviously in, and I can assure you, my dear boy, you have made me happy, very happy indeed."

"I am glad about that," the Marquis replied, "and I would like to see Lady Lavinia before I leave, As you will understand, I must not keep Her Majesty waiting."

"Of course, of course! I must send for Lavinia!" the Duke said fussily.

Realising he had sent the Butler for champagne, he did not ring the bell but opened the door and went out into the passage.

The Marquis heard him shouting for a footman.

He rose from the chair in which he had been sitting.

He went to the window to look out over the garden which was by no means as well-kept as his own.

He was thinking that this was the beginning of a long sequence of events, and he would hate every one of them.

There would be engagement parties for both families.

There would be consultations with Solicitors over the Marriage Settlement.

Endless arguments over the arrangements being made for the wedding.

And when it finally took place, it would be to his mind, a nightmare.

He had been the Best Man at several weddings, and had felt each time that they were completely uncivilised.

There was the sniggering congregation, the envious Bridesmaids trailing dismally along behind the Bride.

The Bridegroom looking dissipated because he had drunk too much the night before.

This would all be followed by the boredom of the Wedding Reception.

44

Hundreds of hands to be shaken, hundreds of congratulations to be answered, hundreds of insincere Good Wishes to be replied to.

Then there was the business of driving away.

He would be showered with rice and rose petals beside a young woman who was almost a complete stranger.

He had seen it happen over and over again.

Because the marriage had been 'arranged' there was little or no love between the Bride and the Bridegroom.

He had either been caught by an ambitious mother, or forced by his family to take a wife so as to produce an heir.

The Bride had been paraded like a horse at a Fair before the highest bidders.

The whole business makes me sick! the Marquis said to himself disgustedly.

Aware that the Duke had come back into the room he turned from the window.

"It is unfortunate, most unfortunate," the Duke was saying, "but Lavinia has gone riding. Apparently she left before I sent a message to say you were calling."

The Marquis was relieved.

"Then I must be on my way," he said, "and perhaps as I am returning to Rake the day after tomorrow, I could call on you and Lady Lavinia some time during the afternoon?"

"Come to luncheon, my dear boy," the Duke cried. "We shall be delighted to see you."

He paused. Then before the Marquis could reply he added:

"Perhaps it would be better, as things are, if I had a little talk with Lavinia before she meets you."

He paused again before continuing:

"She is very shy and has been living very quietly since her mother died. In fact she has not met any young men this past year."

"I understand," the Marquis said, "and of course it would be wise if you had a talk with her."

"She will be delighted at the idea of marrying you," the Duke said reassuringly.

"I shall be looking forward to seeing Your Grace again on Friday," the Marquis said with an effort.

He walked towards the door.

As the Duke followed him they saw the Butler hurrying towards them with a bottle of champagne in an ice bucket.

"Too late!" the Duke said. "His Lordship has to leave immediately."

The Butler stood aside to let them pass.

As they did so, the Duke turned to say in what he thought was a whisper, but was in fact perfectly audible to the Marquis:

"Do not draw the cork! The bottle is not now wanted!"

The Marquis with a feeling of relief, got into his Curricle.

He drove away.

He had the feeling that because he had missed Lady Lavinia he had escaped something which would undoubtedly have proved embarrassing.

He knew only too well that she would have been overwhelmed at the idea of becoming his wife.

At the same time, it would be best for her father to prepare her for the honour.

He thought too, that when he actually proposed to her they should be alone.

After all, it was what any woman would expect.

He vaguely remembered one of his friends saying that when he proposed he had also presented his future Bride with an engagement ring.

"I will get one out of the safe," the Marquis thought.

There was a variety of rings of every sort amongst the Rakemoore collection of jewellery.

He knew too, that his mother's engagement ring was there.

It was a very pretty one with a large diamond cut in the shape of a heart, encircled by smaller diamonds.

He remembered that his father had been very much in love with his mother and she with him before they actually became engaged.

"I fell in love with your father the moment I saw him!" his mother had told him when he was a small boy. "He was the most handsome man I had ever seen! But because I was so young and your father had the reputation of being a Rake, I thought he could never love me!"

"But he did, Mama!"

"Yes, he did. He fell in love with me when we danced together at a Ball given by my father," his mother related. "He asked me as a 'duty dance'. Then when the music stopped we very daringly went out into the garden. It was something considered rather improper in those days!"

"Then what happened?" the Marquis had enquired.

His mother smiled.

"We stood under a tree that was hung with Chinese lanterns and your father said:

'You are the most beautiful person I have ever seen, and I think I must be dreaming!' "

"And then you became engaged," the Marquis prompted.

"Several weeks later," his mother answered, "and by then we were quite certain that we could not live without each other."

There was a tender look in her eyes as she added:

"And just like a Fairy Story, we lived happily ever after!"

Now, as he remembered what his mother had told him, the Marquis could hear her voice softening as she spoke.

There was no doubt they had been very happy.

So happy that it seemed cruel that she should have died

and left her husband inconsolable, and a son who had missed her unbearably.

He wanted to feel her arms around him.

He had cried when she no longer came to kiss him good-night, although he tried not to show his feelings in the daytime.

He realised how much his father was suffering.

He hoped he would never have to suffer in the same way.

His father had been a changed man.

He supposed when he thought of it, that he had been afraid of a love that would hurt him so violently.

The Marquis soon found there were plenty of women who were only too willing to comfort him.

But what they offered him was something very different.

It was not the love he had given and received from his mother.

He knew now he would never find that again.

The Marquis stopped for luncheon.

He reached Windsor exactly a quarter-of-an-hour before he was due for his audience with the Queen.

As he drove up to the Castle he was thinking that he was extremely grateful to Peregrine.

He had saved him from coming here completely unprepared for what Her Majesty had planned.

He hoped he would have enough self-control not to tell The Queen she had no right to interfere in his private life.

At the same time, it might be a near thing.

To be exiled from Court would be a humiliation not only to himself, but also to his whole family.

A Gentleman-in-Waiting took him through a number of long passages to an Anteroom.

He was a man the Marquis disliked, and he had the idea that he knew why he had been sent for.

There was a note in his voice and an expression in his eyes which told the Marquis that the Gentleman-in-Waiting was smirking.

He was, in fact, delighted at the idea of him being 'taken down a peg or two'.

It would, he thought, be just retribution for having been too successful for too long.

"I am sure Her Majesty will not keep you waiting, My Lord," he was saying with mocking civility. "I know she is looking forward to your visit."

"As I am looking forward to seeing Her Majesty," the Marquis replied slowly. "I have something of importance to tell her."

He saw a puzzled expression on the Gentleman-in-Waiting's face.

He thought with a feeling of triumph that he had him worried.

Those who waited on the Queen were so afraid of her and so over-subservient that the Marquis had always despised them.

He thought now that he held a trump card in his hand.

If he surprised everybody, it would serve them right for trying to 'pull a fast one' on him.

He waited for over ten minutes.

"Her Majesty will receive you, My Lord," another *Aide-de-Camp* finally announced in a low voice.

He spoke as if he were in Church.

The Marquis walked slowly and with dignity across the room towards the door.

He was conscious of being received by a woman who represented the greatest Empire in the whole world.

She was in the over-furnished Sitting-Room that he had seen so often before.

There were over two hundred photographs in silver frames arranged on every available piece of furniture.

The Queen was sitting in her favourite armchair.

Draped in black, she looked old and small.

Yet the Marquis knew that one steely glance from her eyes could make the strongest Statesman shiver in his shoes.

"The Most Noble the Marquis of Rakemoore, Your Majesty!" the *Aide-de-Camp* announced.

The Marquis advanced slowly towards her.

When he reached the Queen she held out her hand and he kissed it.

"How are you, My Lord?" she asked.

She was smiling and her eyes were appraising him as he bowed before her.

He was well aware that she liked handsome men.

What she disapproved of was what she called his 'raffish behaviour'.

"It is exceedingly gracious of Your Majesty to receive me," the Marquis said, "and I was in fact, going to ask, Ma'am, for an audience either today or tomorrow, as I have something of importance to tell Your Majesty.'

The Queen looked surprised.

"And what is that?"

"I thought, as Your Majesty has honoured me by being my Godmother," the Marquis replied, "I should inform you, Ma'am, before anybody else, that I am engaged to be married!"

If he had meant to startle the Queen, he succeeded.

Her eyes widened and her eyebrows went up.

"Engaged?"

Her voice was sharp.

"Yes, Ma'am, and I am sure Your Majesty will approve of my choice."

There was a little pause before the Queen asked:

"Who is she?"

"The Duke of Cumberworth's daughter – Lady Lavinia Worth."

There was silence.

The Marquis knew that the Queen was trying to think of some reason why she could oppose the marriage.

Then, almost as if the words were dragged from her, she said:

"I suppose I must congratulate you!"

"I would be deeply disappointed, Ma'am, if you did not do so,"

"I heard that your horse and the Duke's were a dead heat yesterday at Epsom," the Queen said, "but I did not know there was any closer bond between your two families."

"Our estates march together," the Marquis replied, "and it seems a sensible idea that Lady Lavinia and I should be united."

"Sensible!" the Queen exclaimed. "You think of marriage as being a sensible matter?"

"Yes, of course, Ma'am."

The Queen looked at him and her eyes softened.

"I can only hope, my dear Marquis," she said, "that you will be as happy as I was with the Prince Consort."

There was a slight tremor in her voice that was always there when she spoke of Prince Albert.

"I naturally hope the same," the Marquis replied.

He could not help a mocking note creep into his voice as he spoke.

The Queen looked at him sharply.

"It is time you settled down," she said. "I was thinking of appointing you, if you were married, as Lord Lieutenant of your County. As you well know, if you represent me, your reputation must be above reproach."

"I should be very honoured, Ma'am, to be considered for the position," the Marquis said.

He knew as he spoke that it was another way of tying him down.

To make him responsible and prevent him from enjoying himself as he had been able to do as a bachelor.

"I shall consider it," the Queen said, "*after* you are married."

She accentuated the word 'after'.

The Marquis merely bowed his head.

Then, as if she felt the interview had been a waste of time, the Queen held out her hand.

"Goodbye, Marquis," she said. "I shall look forward to hearing about your wedding."

"Your Majesty is most kind," the Marquis said.

He kissed the Queen's hand, then backed slowly from her presence.

She did not watch him go.

He was quite certain she was already considering to whom she could marry the Princess Greta, now that he was no longer available.

In the Anteroom the *Aide-de-Camp* whom he disliked was waiting.

"Your interview was a very short one!" he remarked.

He was obviously curious, and the Marquis replied.

"It was long enough to tell the Queen my good news."

He saw the surprise in the *Aide-de-Camp*'s face and walked off without further comment.

The *Aide-de-Camp* who was obviously in charge hurried to catch up with him.

They did not speak until they reached the door into the Courtyard.

The Marquis' Curricle was waiting outside.

The horses had been changed for another team.

Then he held out his hand.

"Goodbye," he said to the *Aide-de-Camp*, "and thank-you for looking after me so attentively!"

As he strode away the *Aide-de-Camp* stood in the doorway looking after him with a vexed expression on his face.

It gave the Marquis some satisfaction to think he had left the man's curiosity unsatisfied.

He was uncertain and apprehensive as to what had occurred during his interview with the Queen.

At the same time, the Marquis knew that this was only the beginning of a new saga in his life.

He was certain of one thing and one thing only:

The road he was treading was downhill and not up.

At the end of it, there would be only disappointment.

And even worse – the thick fog of unutterable boredom.

Chapter Three

Ila was riding through the woods thinking that they were more magical than ever.

She adored the Spring when the leaves were small and green, and the first primroses and violets appeared amongst the moss.

In fact, to her, the woods were perfect at any time of year because they were so beautiful and part of her thoughts, her dreams and her heart.

Ever since she had been a tiny child she yearned to go to them whether she was happy or unhappy.

The trees welcomed her, the birds, the rabbits, the squirrels and other small animals were more familiar than her friends.

Sometimes she tried to translate into music the sound the wind made in the trees, the humming of the bees and the soft whispers which came from the undergrowth.

Today she was felling particularly happy though there was no obvious reason for it.

She wanted to ride on indefinitely until the woods ended.

Then she would be in the sunshine which would become part of her very breathing.

But she knew there would be a fuss if she did not return, and reluctantly she turned her horse.

She was riding *Swallow* who had been hers ever since he was a foal.

She loved him, she thought, more than anything else in the world.

When she talked to *Swallow* he seemed to understand.

When they were alone in the woods she felt that he too heard what she did. The gnomes working in the caves under the trees. The nymphs swimming in the dark pools, the fairies flitting from flower to flower as if they were butterflies.

Because Ila was younger than her sisters, she had always lived in a world of her own.

It was a world of beauty.

If there were people in it, they were Knights in shining armour, riding out to protect those who were oppressed.

Ila had been christened Lavinia.

When she was quite small her mother the Duchess had told her to say:

" 'I am Lavinia!' "

The child had tried, but all that came from her lips was: "I . . la."

"Try again," the Duchess insisted.

"I . . la, I . . la, I . . la," she repeated.

The three letters were joined together and 'Ila' became the name by which she referred herself.

Her sisters called her Ila, but the Duke refused.

"I will not allow pet names in my family!" he said firmly. "It is common like Billie, Jimmie, Kittie and Bennie!"

As Bennie was the stableboy they had all laughed.

The Duke insisted that his third daughter was addressed as Lavinia, but Ila renamed herself 'Ila'.

If her sisters were pretty, as they undoubtedly were, she was lovely in a very different way.

She was slim and not very tall.

Her eyes dominated her small pointed face.

They were the green of the leaves of the trees and flecked with the gold of the sun.

They were very expressive, eloquent eyes, and yet they seemed to hold a secret which she kept hidden in her heart.

Ila was wearing a riding habit, but no hat, and her hair was the colour of the sun.

Not the sun of the early morning, but when it was burning with the heat of the day.

It was the colour that Botticelli had tried to portray in several of his famous pictures.

Everybody who looked at Ila's hair looked again because it was so unusual.

She was, however, completely unconscious of her looks.

She never thought of them when she glanced in a mirror to see that her hair was tidy.

If it were not, she would receive a reprimand from her father.

He was very critical where his children were concerned.

But both her two sisters, Phyllis and Clementine, were now married and she was alone at the Castle with the Duke.

This last year, since her mother died, he had been more dictatorial than ever.

Ila understood it was because he wished to assert his authority.

There was no one but herself to obey him.

It had been a very quiet year as far as she was concerned, although that did not trouble her.

Her father left to watch his horses run at various Race Meetings.

The house in London was not to be reopened until the end of the month.

Then Ila would start her season as a débutante.

Her Aunt, the Countess of Doncaster, was to chaperon her.

The Duke was already planning that they would have

a small Ball in London in June, and in July a very much larger one in the country.

Ila thought it would be exciting to have some new clothes, and perhaps to meet interesting people.

Her father's friends were interested only in horses.

While she loved horses and especially *Swallow*, she often thought it would be interesting to talk to politicians, artists and musicians.

Perhaps more than anything else she thought she would be interested in meeting Historians.

There were so many things she wanted to know.

Although Worth Castle had a very extensive Library the books were seldom moved from their shelves except by herself.

Only she enjoyed the fascinating world she had found in books which described life in the past.

Her second favourites were the volumes produced by travellers.

She had read them until she felt as if she herself had travelled all over the world.

She had climbed the Himalayas and sailed up the Nile.

She had been fascinated by a book which described a pilgrimage to Mecca.

She had been thrilled by one written by a man who had entered Tibet in disguise and had actually caught a glimpse of the Dalai Lama.

"If I had been born a boy I would be able to do those things," Ila sighed.

She knew it was a bitter disappointment to her father that he had no son.

When she was small she had cried when he had appeared to deal more harshly with her than with her sisters.

Her mother had put her arms round her and explained:

"You have to understand, dearest, that when you were

born Papa was hoping for a boy, and was bitterly disappointed both with me and you."

"Why, Mama?"

"Because he had made up his mind that his third child would be a son and heir, and it meant so much to him."

"Does Papa not love me?" Ila asked.

"Of course he loves you," her mother answered. "It is just that he wanted a boy to ride and hunt with him."

She sighed before she continued:

"He wanted him to accompany him to Race Meetings, and when he died, to take his place in the House of Lords."

As she had grown older, Ila had understood how upsetting it was for her father.

The title would go to a nephew he had never liked and who preferred to live abroad rather than in England.

Because she loved and admired her father, it made her express her affection for him more demonstratively than she would have done otherwise.

She knew now that she was grown-up how pleased he was that she looked so attractive.

He was looking forward to her being a success when she went to London.

"It will be interesting in a way," she said aloud to *Swallow*, "but I shall miss riding you every morning, even though we will come home frequently, if only for Papa to see his mares, and of course, *Ladybird*."

When her father had returned last night from the races he had called the whole stable together.

He had told them all what a success *Ladybird* had been.

Then he had ordered a barrel of ale from which they would drink to future wins.

Then she and her father had dined together, and he had talked of nothing else.

Before she had gone to bed, Ila had kissed him and said:

"I am so very, very glad about *Ladybird*, Papa, as I know how happy it has made you."

"*Ladybird* caused a sensation which will not be forgotten for a long time!" the Duke replied, "and that is what you will be, my dear."

He kissed her cheek before he added:

"I want to hear every man in London acclaiming you, and that is exactly what I believe will happen!"

Ila laughed.

"You are too ambitious, Papa! I will try not to fail you. But do not expect too much."

"You will not fail me," the Duke replied. "You are far prettier than either of your sisters, and when they were presented at Court they eclipsed all the other débutantes."

"I shall just have to hope that I am as lucky as *Ladybird*!" Ila said.

She had gone upstairs to her room.

Only when she was in bed did she wonder if, after all, she really wanted to be a sensation.

She felt it was something that would be rather frightening.

Actually she would be happier in the woods with the birds and the music of the breeze.

Then she sighed.

"I must not disappoint Papa," she told herself, "even though it will seem like entering me for a race in which he wants me to be the winner."

Now as she rode back towards the Castle, she felt perhaps her father would be angry that she had not had breakfast with him.

That meant he would have to go to the stables, which he did every morning, without her.

When she reached the end of the wood she gave *Swallow* his head.

He galloped full out over the flat ground which led to the Park.

There he had to go a little slower because of the rabbit holes under the oak trees.

Ila rode into the stable yard and Bennie the stable boy came forward to lead *Swallow* into his stall.

"'Ad a good ride, M'Lidy?" he asked.

"It was wonderful!" Ila answered in her soft voice.

She patted *Swallow* who nuzzled against her.

Then as Bennie took him away she ran to a side door of the Castle.

She hurried along a corridor and was about to go to the Breakfast-Room when her father came out of his Study.

"There you are, Lavinia!" he exclaimed. "You are late!"

"I know, Papa, and I am sorry. I went further than I intended."

"I want to speak to you, Lavinia."

"I am just going to have my breakfast," Ila replied.

"It can wait for what I have to tell you."

She looked at him a little apprehensively, but he was smiling.

She thought that whatever he had to tell her he was pleased about it.

She followed him into the Study and shut the door behind her.

Then she put up her hands to smooth down her hair.

She thought a little belatedly that it must be untidy from the wind when she was galloping.

The Duke stood in front of the fireplace.

"I have some news for you, Lavinia," he said, "and it is very good news indeed!"

"What is it, Papa?"

"I have just had a visit from the Marquis of Rakemoore!"

Ila's eyes lit up.

"He has agreed to let his stallion serve our mare?"

She knew it was something for which her father had been longing.

"He has agreed to do that," the Duke said with satisfaction, "and he also asked my permission to pay his addresses to you!"

Ila stiffened.

"To do . . what . . Papa?"

"He wishes to marry you," the Duke said, his voice rising, "and I am delighted! Absolutely delighted, Lavinia, to give my permission and accept the Marquis as my son-in-law!"

Ila was frozen into immobility.

She was so shocked by what she had just heard that for a moment she could not think clearly.

The Duke, however, continued in a voice of triumph:

"Rakemoore is not only one of the wealthiest men in the country, he is undoubtedly one of the greatest sportsmen."

He smiled at her before he went on:

"When *Ladybird* achieved a dead heat with Trumpeter yesterday, it suddenly struck me that nothing could be more to our advantage than that you and the Marquis should be married!"

With an effort, Ila found her voice.

"B.but . . Papa . . I have never even . . seen him!"

"He will be calling on you tomorrow afternoon," the Duke said, "and after that your engagement will be announced in *The Gazette*."

He paused a moment and then went on:

"You will have the satisfaction, my dear, of knowing that you have achieved what a great number of other women have failed to do."

"But . . Papa . . " Ila said in a very small voice, "I

have no . . wish to . . marry anybody at the moment . . least of all . . a man I have never . . met!"

"What does it matter whether you have met him or not?" the Duke asked irritably. "You have heard of him. After all, he lives near us!"

"Yes . . Of course I have . . heard of him," Ila agreed slowly.

She was thinking as she spoke of all she had heard about the Marquis.

As far as she was concerned, he had nothing to recommend him, except for his interest in horses.

It was inevitable that he would be talked about incessantly by her father who was envious of his triumphs on the Turf.

He was also gossiped about by everybody in the neighbourhood, including the servants.

Quite a number of the servants at the Castle had brothers and sisters, aunts and uncles, employed by the Marquis.

Everything that went on at Rake was sooner or later disussed, criticised and doubtless exaggerated at the Castle.

Ila had not been particularly interested.

She had never seen the Marquis.

He did not hunt with her father's foxhounds, but preferred the much smarter and better-known packs in Leicestershire.

It was where he had a Hunting Lodge.

He did not turn up at the ordinary events in the County, of which her mother and father had been continual supporters.

Therefore to Ila, he had just been a person who loomed like a genie over the land which bordered theirs.

She had heard about him ever since she was a child.

First when her Nanny whispered about him to the Housekeeper or the housemaids.

She had known by the way they stopped talking when she appeared that they were discussing what the Marquis had just done.

Invariably it was something that was considered outrageous.

Usually it would be about a party he had given.

She thought vaguely, although it did not concern her, that what was being whispered had to do with women.

She would hear their names mentioned and found some of them familiar.

Others were pronounced in a manner which, when she was older, made her think they were actresses.

Or else they were in some way she did not understand, disreputable.

It had obviously been suggested that the Marquis should marry either of her sisters.

Now, after what her father had said, she felt as if she had been hit on the head with a hammer.

She could only stare at him, trying to collect her thoughts.

"It is quite obvious to me that my luck is in!" the Duke was saying. "First *Ladybird*, and now you! If any man has brought off a coup, that is certainly what I have done!"

He was metaphorically rubbing his hands together and crowing like a cockerel.

Ila forced herself to face reality.

"I am . . sorry, Papa," she said in a low voice, "but . . I have no . . wish to . . marry the Marquis of Rakemoore . . and when he comes here tomorrow . . I shall . . refuse him!"

"You will do what?" the Duke asked.

He was so astonished that he did not raise his voice.

Then, as he realised what she had said, he exclaimed in a louder tone:

"You must be out of your mind! Of course you will

63

marry Rakemoore! You ought to go down on your knees and thank God that I have found for you the biggest matrimonial catch in the country!"

"But . . Papa . . when I marry . . I want it to be for . . love!"

"Love! Love!" the Duke exclaimed. "That is all women think about! Love will come after marriage, my dear."

He stopped speaking for a moment before he went on:

"As a multitude of women have broken their hearts over Rakemoore, I am betting on a certainty when I say that you will do the same!"

"I will . . see him, Papa," she said, "but I will certainly not promise to marry him until I know him well, and perhaps . . not even then!"

The Duke lost his temper.

"You stupid little chit!" he shouted. "Do you not understand that you cannot play 'fast and loose' with a man like Rakemoore?"

His voice seemed to quiver with rage as he went on:

"You will accept him quickly in case he changes his mind, and I will hurry you up the aisle for the same reason!"

The Duke went red in the face, and his voice echoed round the room.

"I . . I am sorry, Papa . . ." Ila began.

"If I hear any more nonsense," the Duke roared, "and if you do not do as I tell you, I will beat you until I put some sense into your head!"

He sounded so ferocious that Ila instinctively took a step backwards.

At the same time she was astonished.

He father had never laid a hand on her sisters or herself.

As if he could not contain his anger, the Duke went on:

"I want Rakemoore as a son-in-law, and I want to use his stallion. I am damned if I will have you turning up your nose at the most prestigious husband you, or any other half-witted débutante is likely to get!"

Ila tried to speak, but he continued:

"Anyway it is not a question of whether or not you will marry Rakemoore. You *will* marry him, and as soon as it can be arranged, even if I have to drag you insensible to the altar! Is that understood? And do not dare to argue with me!"

Ila did not reply.

She merely turned and ran from the room leaving her father talking to himself.

She ran up the stairs to her bedroom, shut the door and flung herself down on the bed.

She could hardly believe, even though she was trembling, that she had really heard what her father had said to her.

She knew if he was determined she would marry the Marquis, then there was nothing she could say that would make him change his mind.

He had always been a very obstinate man.

Her mother, whom he had loved, had had the greatest difficulty at times in getting her own way.

Sometimes even she had failed.

"How can I make Papa . . believe that this is something I . . cannot do?" Ila asked despairingly.

She could understand in a way how much it meant to him.

He had always been extremely envious of the Marquis' horses.

Every new addition to his stables was relayed to the grooms at the Castle.

It was Rakemoore who could bid higher for those which were sold in Tattersall's Salesrooms.

It was Rakemoore who bought horses from his friends before anybody else knew they were for sale.

It was Rakemoore who swept past the winning-post at every Race Meeting which the Duke had entered.

The beating of her heart subsided a little.

She was no longer trembling.

But Ila knew that to have the Marquis as his son-in-law would be so greatly to her father's advantage that he would have insisted on the marriage, whatever the bridegroom had been like.

If she was honest, she had to admit that he was certainly better than the husbands who had been provided for her two sisters.

Even to think of their marriages made her so unhappy that she wanted to cry.

It was Phyllis who had suffered first.

She had fallen in love when she was seventeen with a young Squire who lived only a few miles away from the Castle.

They had met out hunting, and although they had known each other since childhood, both of them had lost their hearts.

The Squire came from an old and respected family and owned a very pleasant, if not imposing house and a small estate.

Before she could speak to the Duke, however, disaster fell.

Phyllis went to London to make her curtsy at Buckingham Palace and to attend the first Balls to which she had been invited.

At the very first Ball she met the Duke of Northumbria.

He was a man of over forty and a widower who was looking for a young and atractive wife to give him a son and heir.

Almost before Phyllis knew what was happening her father had approved the alliance.

Everything was arranged before she could go back to the country to tell Geoffrey what had happened.

To say that she and her husband were unsuited was to put it mildly.

Phyllis herself was in despair.

Ila had only been fifteen at the time, but she had to talk to somebody, and Clementine was away at Finishing School.

She had sat on Ila's bed crying and saying over and over again:

"How can I marry that old man when I love Geoffrey. You know I love Geoffrey! Oh, Ila, what can I do?"

She tried speaking to her father and her mother, but both of them thought they were doing their best for their daughter.

Certainly it was for the best from a social point of view.

"You will be a Duchess like your mother," her father kept saying, "and although I think you are pretty enough to attract someone of importance I did not realise there was a Duke available!"

"He is not available to me!" Phyllis had cried to Ila. "He is old and pompous, and when he tries to kiss me, I want to scream!"

But there was nothing she could do.

It was Ila who had kept watch when she had crept out one night to meet Geoffrey in the shrubbery to say goodbye to him.

Phyllis had stumbled back into the Castle and back to her bedroom in the early hours of the morning.

She was as white as a ghost, and so miserable that Ila had to help her into bed.

She became the Duchess of Northumbria in the village Church, where all three sisters had been christened.

The whole County turned up to give far more expensive presents than if she had married somebody of less importance.

They exclaimed over and over again how lucky she was.

The Duke had carried her off to the North of England and Ila had not seen her sister for a year.

She came home for a few days while her husband attended various appointments in London.

To Ila she was no longer the sister she remembered.

She seemed to have forgotten how to laugh.

There was a bitter note in her voice that had never been there before.

"Are you very unhappy, Phyllis?" Ila had asked when they were alone.

"I cannot talk about it," Phyllis had said in a dead tone. "Do you ever see Geoffrey?"

"He meets me when I am out riding to ask if there is any news of you," Ila said.

Phyllis did not speak, and she went on:

"If you would like to write to him or give me a message . . . ?"

Phyllis shook her head.

"What is the point?" she asked.

Ila put her hand over her sister's.

"I am so sorry, dearest," she whispered.

"I am sorry for myself, and I am also sorry for my husband."

Ila had guessed why.

"You are not having a baby?"

"There is no sign of one," Phyllis replied, "and I think he is beginning to hate me because I have not given him what he wants."

She had gone back to the North.

A year later she had had a child, and it had been a daughter.

Ila had not seen the baby, but she had heard that it was not strong.

Phyllis too was weak after what had been a long and difficult confinement.

She had the unhappy feeling that there might not be any more children.

Then the Duke would be even more angry with her sister than he was already.

Clementine had also made an important marriage the year before their mother died.

She had been a great success the first two months of the Season.

She had received half-a-dozen proposals from young men, none of whom the Duke had considered good enough for his daughter.

"I am not in love with any of them," Clementine had said, "so I do not really mind when Papa sends them away with what he calls 'their tails between their legs'!"

She had laughed. Then she went on;

"At the same time, it does seem as if they are proposing to Papa rather than to me, and he appears not to understand it is me who has to marry one of them!"

"Perhaps you will fall in love with somebody of whom Papa does approve," Ila said hopefully.

"I would not want anyone as old as Phyllis's husband," Clementine replied.

The Prince was certainly not as old as the Duke, but he was pompous and very puffed up with his own importance.

He was heir to a small Grand Duchy in the North of Germany.

Ila took a dislike to him from the moment they met.

He made it quite clear that while he professed to be in love with Clementine, and admire her, he thought he was condescending in marrying beneath him.

After all, she was an English girl who was not of Royal blood.

"I do not want to marry him, Papa!" Clementine had protested.

The Duke had pointed out that it was a very important position she was offered.

Even though the Grand Duchy was very small and not of any real importance amongst the Crowned Heads of Europe, she would be treated as a Princess.

She might eventually become the reigning Grand Duchess of her husband's small, mountainous country.

She had returned to England last year for her mother's Funeral.

She had stayed for only two nights at the Castle, but Ila had managed to see Clementine alone.

"Are you happy, Clementine?" she asked.

"Happy?" Clementine said ruefully. "How can I be happy stuck amongst all those fat Germans who eat and talk, talk and eat, and seem to think of nothing else!"

"Is it really as bad as that?" Ila asked.

"It is worse!" Clementine replied.

"But you have a son," Ila persisted thinking of poor Phyllis who had disappointed her husband by giving him a girl.

"Yes, I have a son," Clementine answered. "But I am not allowed to bring him up the way I want to."

She gave a deep sigh before she continued:

"He is surrounded by Nurses who tell me when I may and may not see him, and who disapprove of everything I suggest because it is English rather than German."

"It sounds awful!" Ila said sympathetically.

"It is!" Clementine answered. "What is more, I am forced to spend my life with women – old women who have nothing to do but talk about each other."

She paused a moment before she continued:

"There are deputations of them who expect me to sit and listen at their endless meetings where, as far as I can make out, the result is they do nothing."

"But surely your husband loves you?" Ila asked.

Clementine shrugged her shoulders.

"He is proud of me because everybody says I am beautiful, but I often ask myself what is going to happen when I am not."

"I am sure, dearest, it must be better than you say it is!" Ila cried.

"If anything – it is worse!" Clementine said.

She put her arms around her sister and held her close to her.

"Listen to me, Ila," she said, "you must not marry anyone you do not love. You saw what happened to Phyllis, and you see what has happened to me! Now that Mama is dead, you will have to look after Papa and make him more sensible."

She gave a deep sigh.

"If I had known what marriage was like, I would have thrown myself into the Thames rather than marry Otto."

She had gone back to Germany after the Funeral looking very beautiful.

At the same time, like Phyllis, the laughter had gone from her eyes, and her lips drooped.

In her bedroom Ila put her hands up to her face.

"If I agree to what Papa wants," she told herself, "I shall be like them!"

All the next week she prayed fervently to her mother to save her.

She had known that she had been unhappy about Phyllis.

But even she could not persuade her husband, that the Duke was not a desirable husband, whatever his age.

Ila knew she had also been unhappy about Clementine.

But again her father had been determined that his second daughter should also make a suitable marriage.

Of course it had been brilliant from a social point of view, but at the expense of her sister's happiness.

"I will not marry the Marquis!" Ila told herself.

She heard her own voice and thought it sounded rather weak and frightened.

Then as she lay down she imagined herself riding through the woods on *Swallow*.

She was seeking the happiness she had felt this morning before the bombshell had been dropped.

"What shall I do?"

The question seemed to echo and re-echo in her mind.

It was as if she were asking it of the birds, the rabbits, the squirrels and the trees.

She rode on until she reached the pool.

She spoke to the nymphs she was certain were hidden beneath its dark waters.

The pool was very deep and had never been known to run dry.

She asked the nymphs at the bottom of it who came out when the moon was full to dance in its silver rays:

"What shall I do? What shall I do?"

Now Ila was talking to her mother.

She felt almost as if the Duchess were holding her in her arms as she had when she was very small.

"Help me . . Mama!" Ila pleaded.

She was not sure whether it was the wood or her mother who gave her the answer.

It was that she must run away.

The message was so clear that she did not question it.

She only had to think practically and sensibly how she should do so.

She went downstairs at lunch time and found to her relief that her father was entertaining two of his friends.

They had been at the Race Course the previous day and he had invited them to see his horses.

She thought in the excitement of the Marquis' visit he must have forgotten they were coming.

Fortunately, however, he had told the Butler when he

arrived home from Epsom and luncheon was ready for them.

They were men of about her father's age, both Landowners from different parts of the country.

When they were not talking about horse-breeding, they paid Ila compliments.

They were obviously impressed by her appearance and the way she played hostess in her mother's place.

"Your daughter will quite obviously capture the hearts of every young man in London!" she heard one of them say as she left the gentlemen to their port.

Because she was frightened of what her father might reply, she listened to hear his answer.

She could not believe he would say that she was to marry the Marquis!

Although she was sure he was longing to boast about it to somebody.

"Thank you," the Duke replied. "I hope Lavinia will be, as you say, a success, but I assure you I shall be very particular as to whom she marries."

"Judging by your previous record," one of his friends remarked, "it is a pity that the Prince of Wales already has a wife, or perhaps you are aiming for the Angel Gabriel!"

There was laughter at this, and Ila moved away from the door.

She was thankful her father had not told them about the Marquis.

It would be an embarrassment if he had to retract his words when she was no longer to be found.

She spent the afternoon thinking out exactly what she would do.

Finally, she had it all planned.

Her father would be waiting excitedly for the arrival of the Marquis to luncheon.

By that time, she must be far enough away for it to be impossible for him to find her.

When she was not lost in her dreams, Ila could be very intelligent.

She knew it was most important that she should have some money.

That was a difficulty because she seldom went shopping.

Therefore she had little money of her own.

Her father had given her, like her sisters, £50 a year as 'pin money'.

It was for tips for servants, offertories in Church and, occasionally a purchase from the Carrier.

He called at the Castle every week.

On his cart were ribbons, buttons, pins and a whole variety of other goods which delighted the servants.

The £50 a year, however, was paid only monthly.

Because Ila had been in mourning she still had four months of her 'pin money' practically intact.

In fact, she could only remember spending on what she had put into the offertory bag on Sundays.

She was to stay away for some time, perhaps until the Marquis was married to somebody else.

In which case she would want a great deal more.

She had a few pieces of jewellery of her own.

She had received them at Christmas or on her birthday.

She would take the brooches and bracelets as well as the necklaces with her.

Yet she doubted if she would get much for them especially if they had to be sold in the country.

She had no intention of going to London.

She knew that alone and unchaperoned she would be frightened.

She would find some small village where nobody knew her and she could hide.

She might take in sewing, or perhaps find some other kind of employment.

If there was a village School perhaps she could work there.

Alternatively she could look after other people's babies.

There was pea-picking, plum-picking and harvest time when the mothers worked in the fields.

She did not expect she would be paid much for her services.

But at least it would give her some excuse to be there.

She would not remain a stranger about whom they would talk.

Nothing was very clear in her mind except that she had to leave the Castle.

She started to sort out the things she should take with her.

She found something she had forgotten.

It was a necklace she had been given on her seventeenth birthday.

It had been a present from her Godfather, an elderly man who was an admirer of her father's.

He had collected the half-sovereigns of each year since she had been born.

He had then had them strung on a gold chain which she could wear round her neck.

Her mother had considered it rather vulgar.

Ila had therefore never worn it.

She thought now it would be easy to use the half-sovereigns.

It was only a question of having them detached from the chain.

It was, she thought, as if her mother were helping her to be practical on what was a wild effort to escape from the Marquis.

She put three of her thinnest gowns into a shawl.

She packed two nightgowns, stockings and other small necessities.

She decided to wear a riding habit.

She knew she would have to wear it every day if she stayed away in the Winter.

It would be impossible to take anything more.

Swallow could carry the packed shawl for the first part of the journey.

Afterwards she would have to carry it herself.

Every detail of what she had to do seemed to fall into place.

By the time she went downstairs to dinner, she thought her plan of escape was complete.

She had hidden her shawl in the bottom of her wardrobe.

She just added one very thin muslin blouse to match the one she wore with her riding habit.

When she went down to dinner wearing one of her prettiest gowns she realised her father was slightly apprehensive.

He was afraid they would continue the argument which had taken place in the morning.

She asked him if his visitors had appreciated the horses.

He told her with glee that he had arranged to sell them the next two foals that were born, as well as a Yearling.

They were prepared to pay a better price than he usually obtained.

"You have done well, Papa," Ila said, "but you must be careful not to sell anything that might turn out to be another *Ladybird*."

"Trust me to think of that!" the Duke smiled. "On the other hand, we may have quite a number of would-be purchasers calling after my triumph at Epsom!"

"I do hope so, Papa," Ila said.

When they left the Dining-Room together she thought that if they were not careful they might begin to talk more intimately.

She therefore said:

"As I have a headache, Papa, I hope you will excuse me if I go to bed early."

For one minute she thought the Duke would refuse.

Then, as if he remembered that she must look her best tomorrow, he replied;

"No, of course not, my dear. Go and get your 'beauty sleep' and remember that I want you to wear a pretty gown in which to astonish the Marquis when he arrives because you look so lovely!"

"I am sure when he sees me," Ila replied, "he will be thinking of the Beauties of Mayfair, with whom I shall not compare favourably!"

The Duke laughed.

"Trust Rakemoore to choose the best," he said, "which is something he has always managed to do."

He kissed Ila's cheek and she moved away from him.

As he walked towards his Study and she ran up the stairs, she was saying goodbye.

She loved her father, and she had no wish to hurt him.

At the same time, she had to save herself.

Chapter Four

It was just after half-past-six in the morning when Ila went to the stables.

She knew if she went earlier they would think it strange.

Often in the Summer she was up before seven o'clock.

Swallow was saddled for her and she rode off towards the wood.

She had been thinking in the night that if she went to the very edge of the wood which belonged to her father, she could cross on to the Rake Estate.

Then she could go down the hill and through the small villages where she was unknown.

She remembered there was an old Governess of hers who must be nearly eighty and who had a cottage in one village.

The unfortunate thing was that she could not remember the name of the cottage.

But they would know in the shop where Miss Dunkill was living.

At least, if Miss Dunkill was still alive, she would be able to advise her where to hide.

What was important was not to go anywhere near her father's estate.

Because her mother had always looked after the families of the cottagers and everyone else, she would be recognised.

She had it all planned.

She had wrapped the shawl which contained her clothes in paper.

She told the stableboy who saddled *Swallow* to attach it to the back of the saddle.

"I am taking a present to an old woman who is ill," she explained conversationally.

The boy was obviously not interested.

He fixed it as she wanted, and helped her into the saddle.

She thanked him and rode away, going through the Park as she always did.

Then after galloping *Swallow* over the flat land she rode into the wood.

Immediately she sensed that the agitation she had felt since she awoke had begun to subside.

It was as if the wood not only soothed, but also blessed her.

She was quite certain that it was her mother who had answered her plea for help.

She had told her that she must run away.

"When Papa is aware I am really serious about this," she told herself, "then I can come home."

In the meantime, she was not going to take any chances.

The sooner she put as much distance between herself and her father as was possible, the better.

She did not think he would really worry about her until she did not appear at lunchtime.

Then he would have to think of some excuse to placate the Marquis.

As she thought of him she gave a little shiver.

Whatever else he was, she was sure he was overwhelming and stubbornly authoritative like her father.

It was something she felt she could not endure for the rest of her life.

Instead of riding very slowly and listening to the birds

as she usually did, she hurried *Swallow* along the mossy path.

It twisted and turned through the pine trees.

She passed the deep pool where she believed nymphs hid in the daytime.

She rode on towards the very end of the wood.

It was somewhere she did not visit very often.

Usually by the time she had reached the pool, it was time to turn back to breakfast with her father.

It was a very long, thick wood, and she doubted if anybody except herself rode right through it.

Her father had economised on the woodcutters, reducing their number.

The gamekeepers found this wood not so good for pheasants as those on the other side of the estate.

It was a great relief to Ila that there was no shooting in the place she loved so much.

As she emerged out of the thickness of the wood she turned right.

She rode to the end of her father's estate.

She glanced round to see if there was anyone in sight as she crossed the boundary on to Rake land.

There was a small flat field over which she galloped *Swallow*.

Then to her joy she saw another wood very much like her father's.

She knew this would lead her eventually to the place she was seeking.

It was where she could descend into the valley where the villages were located.

She rode first through the trees.

Then she came out again into the sunshine.

As she did so she saw she was even higher than she expected to be, above land that fell out below her.

Vaguely at the back of her mind she remembered years

ago hearing the servants saying there had been a landslide on the Marquis's estate.

Now she saw a rough edge to the land in front of her.

Beneath it there was a cliff of bare stone.

She was aware that she was seeing where the landslide had taken place.

It had happened over five years ago.

She had been twelve or thirteen years old at the time.

There had been a lot of comment about it and her father had talked of Geologists coming to inspect it.

She drew *Swallow* to a standstill.

She knew it would be beyond this point that she must climb down so as to reach the villages she was seeking.

It was also here that she would have to leave *Swallow* and go on alone.

It broke her heart not to be able to take him with her.

But she was sensible enough to know that a horse as outstanding and as fine as *Swallow* would inevitably cause comment.

She therefore rode back the way she had come to where she could see her father's wood only a few hundred yards away.

She dismounted and took her parcel from the back of the saddle.

She lifted the stirrup on to the pommel so that it would not thump against *Swallow's* side.

Then she put her arms around his neck and kissed him.

"I have to leave you now, darling," she said, "but you will be safe at home, and do not forget me until I can come back to you."

Swallow nuzzled against her, and she thought he understood.

Then turning him in the direction in which she wished him to go she said:

"Go home, *Swallow*, go home!"

She had taught him a long time ago to obey her, but

this was a greater request than he had ever undertaken before.

He looked at her as if doubtfully for a moment.

Then as she said again: "Go home!" he started to move away from her.

He was looking ahead towards the wood, as if he knew which way he should go.

"Go home, *Swallow*," she said again.

He set off at a trot and she watched him until she saw him entering the wood.

She waited, just in case he should return.

But she knew, because she had trained him well, that he would find his way back to his own stable.

There were tears in her eyes because she was parting from him.

She wiped them away and picked up her shawl.

She retraced her way to the landslide.

Now as she went to the edge and looked down, she saw why there had been such a fuss about it.

There was a sheer drop of a hundred feet, leaving bare ground which apparently had not been surveyed before.

It was still so sharp and rough that she felt the fall might have happened yesterday.

At the bottom she could see great boulders lying like rocks on a seashore.

There were a few bushes that had grown amongst them, but on the cliff there was no vegetation.

She walked on wondering if any more of the land would fall. If it did, it would be part of the wood.

As the sun was getting hot she moved a little closer to the trees, seeking their shade.

She had come away without a riding-hat because the one she habitually wore was too smart.

The women in the villages did not wear hats, but threw a shawl over their heads.

Anyone walking as she was doing, and wearing a hat, would certainly, she thought, attract attention.

She had put on her oldest riding-habit which looked more like an ordinary suit rather than the latest fashion in habits.

These were tailor-made and severely cut.

The habit she was wearing she had had since she was sixteen.

It therefore had a full skirt under which she wore a starched petticoat.

A loose jacket covered a white muslin blouse.

They were the most unobtrusive clothes she possessed and she only hoped no one would notice her.

She had almost reached the end of the landslide which was on her left when she heard a sound in the wood.

She stopped beneath a tree.

She thought perhaps it would be one of the Marquis's gamekeepers or perhaps a woodcutter.

She hoped frantically that she would not be seen and drew as close as she could to the trees.

It was then she became aware of a path winding into the wood.

It was very much the same as the one which she had ridden with *Swallow*.

When she looked along it she saw what she thought at first was a horse.

Then she realised it was a pony coming down the path, but it was some way away.

Suddenly she was aware that the pony was rearing, bucking and behaving in what seemed a crazy manner.

She stared at it, thinking she must be mistaken.

Then as it came nearer, still behaving in an extraordinary way, she could see there was a small boy riding it.

He obviously had no control over it.

It came nearer still and she expected every moment to see the small boy thrown from the saddle.

But despite being tossed about, he managed to remain seated.

Ila could only stare until the pony made a rush forward and she realised with horror it must be mad.

If it continued twisting and turning as it reared, it would go over the landslide and crash on to the boulders below.

The pony reached the end of the path.

It was then, without even thinking, that Ila dropped her shawl and ran forward.

She flung herself at the pony's head and was only just in time.

It was only about two feet to the edge of the landslide.

As she struggled to hold the apparently demented animal, she shouted to the boy:

"Throw yourself off! Quickly! Quickly!"

He obeyed her.

As he did so the pony reared up again, sending the boy crashing into Ila and knocking her to the ground.

The reins were torn from her hands and the pony disappeared over the edge of the cliff.

Ila, however, was not aware of this.

As she fell with the boy on top of her, she hit the back of her head against a heavy stone.

Robin Moore picked himself up.

Two grooms came from the wood, white-faced at the horror of what they had seen.

"Be ye orl roight, Master Robin?" one of them asked in a shaken voice.

Robin did not answer.

He had raised himself up from Ila and was staring over the cliff.

He could see his pony where it lay at the bottom.

The groom who stood up beside him said:

"'E be dead, Master Robin!"

"He was stung by a wasp," Robin said. "There were two or three of them, and I saw one on his neck."

"There be a 'ole nest o' 'em!" the groom said.

He turned from Robin's side to where the other groom was kneeling to put his arm behind Ila's head.

"Th' Lady saved yer life, Master Robin," he said, "but 'er 'it 'er 'ead on this 'ere stone."

"Has she fainted?" Robin asked.

"Oi thinks 'er be concussed," the older groom replied, mispronouncing the word.

"We shall have to take her back to the house," Robin said, "but it is a long way."

"Oi've got a better idea," the older groom said. "We'll take 'er to t'house in the wood."

"Where is that?" Robin asked.

"It be not far off," the groom replied, "an' Mrs Wilcox'll know wot t'do, 'er were Nanny to 'Is Lordship."

"'Ow us gonna get 'er there?" the other groom asked.

"Us'll carry 'er," the older man said, "an' Master Robin'll lead our 'orses."

"Yes, of course," Robin agreed.

He looked down at Ila lying with closed eyes.

"Be careful how you carry her," he said, "I want to thank her for saving my life."

"If 'er 'adn't . . ." the younger groom began, "ye'd be gon'un . . ."

He stopped as if he thought what he was saying was a mistake.

Robin was handed the reins of the two horses, who were docile animals.

They had been cropping the grass since the grooms had dismounted.

"Us'll go a'ead," the older groom said, "as us knows th' way."

Robin did not reply.

He was watching as the grooms picked Ila up in their arms.

They started to carry her a little awkwardly from the side of the cliff on to the path in the wood.

It was only when they reached it that Robin called out:

"There is a parcel by the tree which she must have dropped when she ran to try and stop *Rufus*!"

The grooms put Ila down again.

The younger groom picked up the shawl from where Robin had seen it.

Tucking it under his arm he went back to where she was lying.

It took some time to move down the path in the wood and then to turn off on to another.

It led them into what seemed to be the very heart of the wood itself.

Then surprisingly there was a clearing which had a view over the countryside.

At the back of it stood a strange-looking house.

Two hundred years earlier the then Marquis of Rakemoore had, when he had grown old, decided to retire from his position.

He left the running of his estate to his eldest son.

The House in the Wood had been used as a Hunting-Lodge by a previous ancestor.

The Marquis had taken it over and had had it made habitable.

He had spent the last years of his life there writing his memoirs.

After that, the house had sometimes been used by keepers.

They kept a watch at night for foxes and other vermin which disturbed the sporting birds.

It was occasionally occupied by the younger members of the family in the Summer.

They used it to picnic on their own, away from paternal authority.

The present Marquis had, however, allowed his old Nanny, when she retired, to live there.

Surprisingly she had decided to marry the Head Gamekeeper.

Wilcox had served the family for forty years and Nanny for thirty.

The Marquis had thought that the least he could do was to let them live out their days in a comfortable cottage.

But Wilcox loved the woods and wanted to continue to be able to 'keep an eye on things'.

They had therefore moved into the House in the Wood and were, apparently, very content.

To everybody else on the estate it seemed isolated and spooky.

When Nanny Wilcox heard the knock on the door she went to open it.

"What has happened?" she asked.

The older groom explained how Ila had saved Robin's life, but had hit her head on a stone.

Almost before he had finished speaking, Nanny opened the door wider and said:

"Come in, and be careful how you carry her down the passage for it's narrow."

The building was one-storeyed.

Nanny led them to a room that was obviously not used although it was clean and comfortable.

The Marquis had ordered that the curtains, carpets and furniture used by his ancestors be restored to the house when Nanny Wilcox moved in.

There was a large, comfortable bed, with curtains falling on each side of it.

A thick carpet lay on the floor and all the furniture had been stored at Rake until it was wanted.

The groom put Ila gently down on the bed.

"Will us be fetchin' the Doctor?" one of the grooms asked Mrs Wilcox.

"If she hit her head on a stone she'll be suffering from concussion," Nanny replied tartly, "and as I've been dealing with that sort of thing all my life, I know what to do!"

The older groom hurried to the front door to see if Robin had followed them safely.

He was standing outside holding the two horses.

The groom took the horses' reins from him and he walked into the house.

He found his way down the passage and into the bedroom.

The younger groom was telling Nanny Wilcox of the mad way the pony had behaved after it had been stung by wasps.

"It were terr'ble!" he was saying, "real terr'ble t' watch! But 'twere nought Jim an' me could do."

"She saved my life," Robin interposed from the door, "so you will have to look after her very, very carefully."

He spoke in his usual aggressive way, but Nanny smiled at him.

"She'll be safe with me," she assured him, "and as I understand it, you're the young gentleman as has come to live at the Big House."

"I am Robin Moore," Robin announced, "and this lady saved my life."

"So I've been hearing," Nanny replied, "and I know you'll want to thank her when she's well enough for you to do so."

"I will wait here until she is," Robin said.

He spoke with a note of aggression in his voice as if he thought Nanny or the grooms would argue with him.

"Well, you're welcome to stay, if that's what you wish," Nanny agreed.

She turned to the grooms.

"You'd better look at that poor pony if it's gone over

the landslide," she said. "If I've said it once, I've said it a dozen times – that cliff ought to have a fence round it."

"That's roight," the older groom said, "it should."

"And you mark my words," Nanny continued, "it'll be done, now that it's too late. It's always the same – talk, talk, talk, but nothing's done 'til something like this happens!"

"As soon as we can get a rope, we must get him back to the stables," Robin said.

The groom shook his head.

"'E be dead, Master Robin. No animal could fall from that 'eight, an' live."

He was thinking as he spoke that Robin could have died too.

Then, as Nanny thought the same thing, she said sharply:

"Now hurry back to the stables and arrange for somebody to come and bury the poor creature."

She paused a moment and then went on:

"You'll also want to take off the saddle and bridle before it's stolen."

"Aye, o' course, Mrs Wilcox, ye're roight," the older groom said.

He moved towards the door, then hesitated.

"Ye be quite sure, Master Robin, ye want t' stay 'ere? Us could come back an' fetch ye later in th' afternoon."

"I am staying until the lady wakes!" Robin said positively.

"Now be off with you," Nanny said.

"'Er 'ad a parcel with 'er," the groom said. "Oi puts it down outside when us reaches yer 'ouse."

"I'll come and fetch it," Nanny answered.

They went from the room and Robin moved nearer the bed.

He stared at Ila.

Then as if he was afraid she might be dead, he touched her hand.

It was not cold, but he was still afraid.

He was wondering whether if he touched her he would feel her heart beating.

Suddenly she opened her eyes.

She did not seem to see him, and she said in a frightened voice he could only just hear:

"Hide . . me . . hide . . me! They . . must . . not find . . me!"

She made a little movement.

Then her eyes closed again and she lapsed into unconsciousness.

The Marquis arrived for luncheon with the Duke at exactly a quarter to one o'clock.

The Duke greeted him effusively.

The Marquis had no idea there had been a tremendous commotion just before he was due.

The Duke had a meeting with his Estate Manager and had gone with him to inspect one of the out-buildings.

On arriving back soon after twelve he expected to find his daughter waiting for him.

She had not appeared at breakfast.

He thought, as she had said she was not feeling well the night before, that she had stayed in bed.

It was very important, he thought, that she should look her best and be well dressed when she met the Marquis.

The Duke was well aware of the Marquis' love affairs.

He knew there had been a great number of them, and that they had all been with sophisticated Beauties.

At the moment London Society abounded with them.

He was convinced that the Marquis' sudden desire to be married had to do with his affair with Lady Wisbourne.

It was, he told himself, an 'ill wind that blows nobody any good'.

Nothing could be more satisfactory than that Rakemoore should be his son-in-law,

When during the night he had thought over Ila's protestations, he told himself it was just nervousness.

Every young woman felt that when she was on the brink of marriage.

"How can she think of anything so foolhardy as refusing the most sought after man in the whole of England?" he asked himself.

It amused him to think of the frustration of the ambitious mothers.

They had tried for years to trap the Marquis into marrying one of their daughters.

"They will be grinding their teeth," the Duke thought with glee, "but there will be nothing they can do about it!"

He decided he would inspect Ila very carefully to see that she looked her best at luncheon.

It was a pity they had not had time to go to London to buy the gowns she would wear during the Season.

Then he remembered that his sister, who was to chaperon her, had sent her only a week ago a gown and a coat in which she could travel.

She had also ordered several other gowns.

Ila could wear those until they found the time to visit the Bond Street Dressmakers.

"That is satisfactory," the Duke said to himself.

He remembered that his sister's taste was impeccable.

As soon as he entered the front door he said to the Butler:

"Tell Lady Lavinia I want to see her immediately in my Study."

"Very good, Your Grace."

A footman was dispatched upstairs to look for Her Ladyship while the Butler went first to the Library.

He knew she was more likely to be there than anywhere else.

It was ten minutes later before they reported to the Duke that Lady Lavinia was nowhere to be found.

"What do you mean – nowhere to be found?" the Duke shouted angrily. "She must be somewhere in the house! If not, she is in the stables! You fools! Find her and tell her to come here at once!"

He thought with fury that it was like Lavinia to be messing about with the horses.

She should be dressing herself in readiness for the Marquis.

When he was told she was not in the stables either, he grew crimson in the face with anger.

"She must be somewhere!" he roared. "Search the whole house!"

"We have already done so, Your Grace."

"Then search it again! Her Ladyship must be either in the attics, the cellars or the kitchens."

He was told that the Marquis' Curricle was coming up the drive.

It was then he realised that Lavinia was deliberately hiding herself.

He grew so angry that the Butler was afraid he would have a stroke.

But the Duke knew that the most important thing was not to let the Marquis know what had happened.

He therefore forced himself to smile and say as they entered the Study:

"I am extremely sorry to tell you that you will not be able to meet Lavinia today, as I had expected you to do."

The Marquis raised his eyebrows.

"She is not here?"

"I am afraid not. In fact, I had forgotten," the Duke replied, "that she had an appointment to see one of our relatives who is not well."

92

He stopped speaking, smiled and then continued:

"She has a very acute sense of duty, and she thought it would be unkind to cancel the arrangement at the last moment."

"I understand," the Marquis said.

"It is annoying," the Duke went on, "but at least, we can talk about our horses, and as soon as luncheon is over, I will take you to see my mares."

The mares were certainly impressive.

As the Marquis drove back to Rake he was thinking that the Duke's enthusiasm was justified.

It might even be possible for them to breed a champion as he was so keen to do.

The Marquis naturally thought it surprising that Lady Lavinia had not been there to meet him.

"I will bring Lavinia over to see you tomorrow, if you are still staying in the country," the Duke said, "or you could come to us."

"I intend to be here until Monday," the Marquis replied, "and of course, you are welcome at Rake at any time."

He was perceptive enough to realise that the Duke was delighted at the idea that the front door of Rake would always be open to him.

He was thinking, however, that talk about mares would begin to pall after a time.

As he drew nearer his home he remembered that he had not asked anybody to stay for the weekend.

He had thought he should concentrate on getting to know Lady Lavinia.

Now he wished that Peregrine Brentwood was waiting for him, and realised also that he would be alone for dinner.

A groom was waiting to take his Curricle to the stables.

He walked into the Hall to find his Secretary Mr Barrett as well as Dawson the Butler waiting for him.

There was an expression on both their faces that told the Marquis before they spoke that something was wrong.

"What has happened?" he asked.

"It's Master Robin, M'Lord," Dawson said.

"What has he been up to now?" the Marquis asked.

It was Mr Barrett who answered him.

"According to the grooms who accompanied him out riding this morning," he replied, "Master Robin nearly lost his life!"

The Marquis was startled.

"What do you mean by that?"

"His pony *Rufus* stepped on a wasps' nest in the wood and went wild. He rushed bucking and kicking through the wood. Master Robin would have been taken down the landslide with him if a woman had not intervened."

The Marquis listened with an incredulous expression on his face.

"Why the Devil did he go near the landslide?" he asked. "Everybody has been warned that it is dangerous!"

"Master Robin was leading the way, My Lord, as he always does, and the grooms were some way behind."

He paused a moment and then said:

"Then they realised what had happened and they had no idea how they could save him."

"But he was saved?" the Marquis asked sharply.

"A young woman checked the pony as it reached the edge of the chasm. She shouted to Master Robin to jump just as the pony went over the edge and was killed!"

The Marquis gave a sigh of relief.

"Thank God the boy is all right. Where is he?"

"The grooms carried the young woman to the House in the Wood as it was quite near, and Master Robin insisted on staying there until he can thank her for saving his life."

The Marquis looked surprised.

He had never known Robin to show politeness ever since he had been in his charge.

He was rude, aggressive and completely uncontrollable with everybody, including himself.

"So Master Robin is at the House in the Wood!" he said to his Secretary.

"Yes, My Lord."

"Then I will go there at once," the Marquis said. "Order *Saracen* while I change into my riding clothes."

He walked up the stairs thinking as he did so that it was typical of his nephew to get himself into some sort of mess.

But he supposed the boy could not help his pony being stung by wasps.

At the same time, why did he want to go into the wood?

There were acres of ground to ride over without moving amongst the trees.

He had also warned everybody that the landslide was dangerous.

He had never thought of a child falling over it.

He had feared that his dogs or the Keepers might take a false step on a dark night.

"I should have erected a fence around it a long time ago," the Marquis told himself.

He rode through the wood thinking how attractive it looked in the afternoon sunshine.

He well knew the way to the House in the Wood.

It had always fascinated him when he had been a small boy.

It had been shut up for years because it was thought that the ghost of his ancestor who had lived there still haunted it.

His old Nanny had had no such qualms.

It was she who had suggested she would like to live there.

Her husband wished to spend his days, although he was retired, looking after the birds.

"That's where I'd like to be, Master Osbert," she said. "I never could stand being cooped up in a village with a lot of old women peering over my fence to see what I'm doing."

The Marquis had laughed.

"You know you can have any cottage you like, Nanny, but I agree, the House in the Wood is the right place for you."

He stopped speaking a moment and then went on:

"Instead of keeping a lot of children in order, I have no doubt you will be teaching the squirrels how to behave and making the rabbits wash their faces!"

Nanny had laughed.

The Marquis thought now how much he owed her for giving him such a happy childhood.

His father and mother had loved him, but they were both very busy people.

It was Nanny who had read him his first Fairy Stories.

It was Nanny who had given him his first lessons.

It was Nanny who had taught him to have responsibility for the people on his estate.

Nanny who had taken him to Church.

They had sat in the family pew, and he had taken his father's place when he was not there.

He behaved, as she put it, 'like a little Gentleman'!

He wondered as he left the house what Nanny would make of Robin, or rather, what Robin would make of Nanny.

"He has been a headache," the Marquis thought, "ever since his mother died."

The Marquis dismounted outside the house.

He tied *Saracen's* reins on his neck, leaving him to wander.

He had had *Saracen* for some years and had taught him to come when he was called.

There was therefore no need to tie him up.

The front door was open and the Marquis walked in.

He looked into the kitchen and found, as he expected, Nanny washing up the tea things.

"Hello, Nanny!"

"Master Osbert!" she exclaimed. "I was thinking you'd be coming to see me with all the excitement we've been having."

"I am thankful that my nephew is all right," the Marquis replied. "Apparently some young woman saved his life."

"She's unconscious, the poor young thing." Nanny said, "and a prettier Lady you've never seen!"

"Lady?" the Marquis questioned. "I thought she would be a Farmer's daughter, or perhaps a girl from the village."

Nanny shook her head.

"Oh, no, Master Osbert, she's a Lady born and bred, you can take my word for it!"

"I never knew you to make a mistake, Nanny," the Marquis smiled, "but what was she doing near the landslide?"

Nanny made an expressive gesture with her hands.

"That's something we'll have to wait to find out when she can speak, Master Osbert!"

"I would like to see her."

"She's in what I calls my 'spare bedroom'," Nanny replied, "and you know where that is."

The Marquis smiled at her.

Then he walked along the passage.

The door into the spare bedroom was ajar and he pushed it open.

He saw Robin standing at the window looking out.

He turned as the Marquis came towards him.

"How is she?" the Marquis asked.

"She is still unconscious, Uncle Osbert," Robin replied in a whisper.

The Marquis walked to the bed.

From all he had heard he was expecting to see a rather hefty young woman.

He was therefore astonished when he looked down at somebody who looked small and almost childlike.

At the same time she was so lovely that he could hardly believe his eyes.

Nanny had undressed Ila.

She had put on one of the lace-trimmed nightdresses from the shawl she had been carrying.

She had taken out the pins in her hair in case they hurt her head.

It must, he thought, be very tender from where she had hit it on the stone.

The fall had, however, luckily not broken the skin.

Now the Marquis saw Ila's red-gold hair falling over her shoulders.

It curled just slightly at the tips.

He recognised it immediately as the colour that Botticelli had used to depict the *Birth of Venus*.

It was a colour the Marquis had never seen on a living woman before.

In the light from the evening sun it looked like flaming gold.

Ila's eyelashes were dark against her cheeks.

She was very pale and the Marquis thought she did not look real.

He thought she could be something that had come from the wood itself and might easily disappear.

Then he told himself he was being imaginative.

As he stood looking at her he realised that Robin was standing beside him doing the same thing.

"Has she spoken at all since she has been here?" he asked.

"Yes," Robin replied in a whisper. "She spoke to me."

"What did she say?" the Marquis asked.

"She said: 'Hide me! Hide me! They must not find me!'"

Robin looked up at him.

"That is what we must do. We must not betray her when she saved me from dying with *Rufus*."

"No, of course not," the Marquis agreed.

"We must not tell anybody at Rake about her," Robin went on, "otherwise the wicked people who are hunting her will come and take her away."

"How do you know they are wicked?" the Marquis asked.

"She would not be running away if they were good!" Robin replied, with what the Marquis thought was surprising logic.

"No, of course not," he agreed, "and therefore, Robin, we will keep her presence here a secret until she can tell us why she is in hiding."

Robin looked at him in what the Marquis thought was a strange way.

"You promise you will not betray her?" he asked.

The Marquis was astonished.

It was the first time he had known Robin to think of anybody but himself.

Ever since he had been at Rake he had only passed from one tantrum to another.

He had driven away his Governesses in despair.

Because the Marquis felt this was a new development which should be encouraged, he said:

"I think in the circumstances, Robin, she is your responsibility. Therefore it is quite right that you should look after her."

"That is what I mean to do," Robin replied. "She held

on to Rufus's reins, and he was rearing up and mad because the wasps had stung him."

"It must have been very frightening," the Marquis observed.

"She said to me: 'Throw yourself off!' " Robin went on, "but when I did so, because *Rufus* was jumping about so much I fell on top of her and she struck her head on a stone."

This was what the Marquis had already heard and he said:

"I do not think she will be concussed for very long, but anyway, Nanny will know what to do."

Robin looked up at the Marquis.

There was an aggressive note back in his voice as he said:

"I am going to stay here with her. I am not coming back to Rake!"

The Marquis thought quickly before he said:

"Of course you must stay, if that is what you wish. We just have to ask Nanny politely if she minds having so many strangers in the house."

"I will be no trouble," Robin promised.

The Marquis was about to say that he had been trouble everywhere else he had been, but he thought it would be a mistake.

Instead, he walked from the bedroom back into the kitchen.

Nanny looked at him with a twinkle in her eyes.

He knew she was aware that he was surprised at how beautiful their unexpected visitor was.

"My nephew wishes to stay here with you, Nanny," the Marquis said, "and if you will undertake to keep him, I think you are the only person who could make him behave himself."

"I've been told he's a bit of a rascal!" Nanny said.

"That is an understatement!" the Marquis replied.

"Well, of course he can stay, if he wants to," Nanny agreed. "It'll give me something to do. I'm getting lazy in my old age!"

"I cannot imagine you doing anything but putting anyone who came into the Nursery in their right place."

Nanny smiled.

"What I'm missing is a Nursery, and when are you going to give me one, I'd like to know?"

"It is something which may happen sooner than you think!" the Marquis said.

"You mean – you are going to be married?" Nanny enquired excitedly.

The Marquis nodded.

Nanny looked at him.

She saw that his eyes had darkened and there was an expression on his face she knew only too well.

Unexpectedly, because she knew him better than he knew himself, she said:

"Well, you must tell me all about it some time. Now we have to concentrate on this young lady, and make her well again."

"Robin has promised he will help you," the Marquis said, "and of course I will send you food and somebody to help you in the house, if that is what you would like."

"I don't need anyone coming here, poking about and talking their heads off," Nanny said. "Master Robin says the young Lady's in hiding, and we'll keep her hidden until we knows what it's all about."

The Marquis laughed.

"It sounds just like the old days, Nanny, and nobody is more capable than you."

He walked towards the door.

"I will come and see you tomorrow. In the meantime if there is anything you want, you have only to ask for it."

"I'll do that, Master Osbert," Nanny replied, "and thank you!"

"I should be thanking you," the Marquis replied. "I am just wondering how you will cope with my nephew. He has driven everybody else crazy."

Nanny laughed, and the Marquis knew it was a challenge she would enjoy.

"There has never been anybody like you, Nanny," he said with a sincere note in his voice, "and as far as I am concerned, there never will be!"

"Get along with you!" Nanny laughed. "That's the sort of flattery those beautiful ladies in London I hear about like to have!"

"I thought living here in the country," the Marquis remarked dryly, "it was only the birds and the rabbits you listened to. What do you know about the 'Beautiful Ladies' in London?"

"What d'you think people talk about here when the work's done?" Nanny enquired. "Just the same as those chattering women at Rake and those poor ageing creatures in your Alms House."

She put the saucepan she had been holding down on the stove as she added:

"And very bad 'tis for you, Master Osbert, to know they thinks you're so important!"

Chapter Five

Thinking it over during the night, the Marquis came to a decision.

It was important that Robin should get back on a pony as soon as possible.

He knew his nephew was an exceptionally good rider.

But what had happened might have upset him to the point where he did not wish to ride again.

He had known this happen where young people had a bad fall.

Or else had been frightened by obstreperous horses.

Soon after breakfast he sent for his Head Groom.

The man told the Marquis that the grooms had already buried *Rufus*.

The Marquis explained to his Head Groom that he thought it important that Robin should ride again as soon as possible.

"Oi were thinkin' that meself, M'Lord," he said "an' a nasty shock it musta bin for th' young gen'man, losin' 'is pony loike that!"

"Have we another pony in the stables?" the Marquis enquired.

"Aye M'Lord, but he's bigger, though quiet-like."

"Very well, tell the groom to follow me with the pony when I go to visit Master Robin this afternoon."

Then as he thought it over he said:

"Send one of the grooms who was with Master Robin

yesterday, and make sure they do not exaggerate what happened."

He paused a moment and then went on:

"I understand Mr Barrett warned them not to make too much of a 'song and dance' about it."

The Head Groom looked embarrassed.

"Oi 'spects they 'ad to explain, M'Lord, why Master Robin ain't returned."

The Marquis knew that, whatever Robin might say, it would be impossible to keep the young woman's presence a secret.

"Have the pony ready in about half an hour," he said sharply, "and I will ride *Saracen*."

"Very good, M'Lord," the Head Groom replied.

All the evening the Marquis found himself wondering who the young lady was, and how she could possibly be so beautiful.

Then he told himself it must be an illusion.

He had seen her in unusual circumstances, and had thought her to be far lovelier than she actually was.

"I expect when I hear her speak," he added, "she will talk with an accent, and Nanny must have been mistaken."

Then he knew mockingly that he was just making excuses for his own curiosity.

Nanny, of all people, would not make a mistake about a person's status in life.

He rode off from Rake a little later.

The groom following him was leading a nice-looking pony which, as the Head Groom had said, was bigger than *Rufus*.

As he drew near to the House in the Wood the Marquis was wondering what had happened on the previous evening.

Robin had behaved so badly wherever else he had been

that he could not help thinking apprehensively that Nanny may have had a shock.

His relatives with whom he had placed the little boy had all been very voluble about him.

They reiterated their horror at his rudeness, his bad language and the amount of things he had broken when he was in a tantrum.

At Rake he had behaved even worse.

He had sworn at his Governesses who had been scandalised by his behaviour.

He had deliberately upset a jug of water over one and an inkpot over another.

They had left immediately.

The Marquis thought it strange that his brother, who had been a particularly charming and good-natured man, should have had such a son.

He could not help wondering if there were a streak of lunacy in the family.

It might be something of which he was not aware.

Yet he himself might in the future be confronted by progeny who behaved in the same manner.

He arrived at The House in the Wood and left *Saracen* to roam free as he had before.

The door was open.

He walked in and found, as he expected, that Nanny was in the kitchen preparing the luncheon.

"Good morning, Nanny!" he said. "How is your patient?"

"Just coming round, Master Osbert," Nanny replied, "and a prettier young lady I've never seen!"

"Who can she be?" the Marquis enquired.

Nanny shrugged her shoulders.

"It's a real mystery!" she replied, "but I knows one thing: she shouldn't be wandering about alone or she'll get into trouble."

The word 'trouble' made the Marquis think of Robin.

"And how has Robin behaved?" he asked.

"Like a perfect gentleman!" Nanny replied.

Her eyes were twinkling as she spoke and the Marquis said:

"If you are telling the truth, Nanny, then I know in ancient times you would have been burned as a witch, as you have obviously put a spell on him!"

"If them as looks after him knew their job," Nanny replied, tartly, "he'd behave well enough."

The Marquis laughed.

"Is he with your patient now?"

"He won't leave her for a minute," Nanny said, "You'd better go and see for yourself."

"That is just what I was thinking of doing," the Marquis smiled.

He left the kitchen to walk along the corridor to the spare bedroom.

He reached the door.

He was just about to knock when he realised it was slightly ajar.

He could hear Robin's voice, and because he was curious, he stayed outside to listen.

"I am so sorry about your pony," a very soft voice said.

"*Rufus* is dead," Robin replied, "but I will not cry for him because it does no good."

"What do you mean – no good?" Ila asked.

There was silence. Then Robin said:

"He is dead, and they will put him in the ground like they put – my mother."

The way he spoke was strange and very bitter in anyone so young.

"So your mother has gone to Heaven," Ila said very gently, "and so has mine."

"She is not in Heaven!" Robin said positively. "That is what they told me, but they put her in a box and buried her in the ground."

He made a little sound that was rather like a sob as he went on:

"I tried to dig her up but they would not let me."

There was silence for a moment, then Ila said:

"Listen, Robin, I have something to tell you."

"What is it?"

"Your mother is not in the ground, only her body is there."

She saw Robin did not understand, and she explained:

"If you wore the clothes you have on for a long time, what would happen to them?"

"They would get old and ragged," Robin replied.

"They would," Ila agreed, "and that is what happens to our bodies. We get old and our body is no use, so we throw it away."

She saw that Robin was listening, and she went on:

"When it is what we call 'buried', we are still alive, in what people call 'Heaven'."

There was silence, then Robin said:

"Did you say – Mama was – alive?"

"Of course she is alive," Ila answered, "and she is looking after you loving you and, when you want her, very, very close to you."

"I do not believe it!" Robin said.

"It is true!" Ila assured him. "If I am worried or unhappy and do not know what to do, I talk to my mother as you can talk to yours."

"How? How can I do that?" Robin enquired.

"When you are alone or feeling upset, talk to your mother. Tell her how much you miss her and how you want her near you."

"And what will happen?" Robin asked.

"You will feel her close to you, and if you listen, not with your mind, but with your heart, she will tell you what to do."

Robin drew a deep breath.

"Is that really true? Cross your heart, and not tell a lie?"

"I swear to you it is true, and it is everything I believe. I promise I do not tell lies."

"And Mama can see me now – at this moment – talking to you?"

"Of course she can, but sometimes she is busy, and therefore you must call her, with what in Church you call a prayer."

Robin thought this over.

"I pray to Mama – and not to God?"

"You pray to both, and if there is anything that worries you or makes you unhappy, you tell your mother about it just as you would if you could see her."

"And she is really there?"

"Of course she is!" Ila said.

"Do you talk to your mother?" Robin asked.

"I talk to her every day and she helps me when I do not know what to do. Do you know what happened?"

"What did?" Robin asked.

"She told me I must run away, and I am quite certain it was your mother who made sure I was in the right place at the right moment when I saved you from falling over the cliff on *Rufus*."

"My Mama told you to stop him?"

"Something told me to, something made me jump up and run towards your pony. When I shouted at you to jump off and you did so, I am certain it was your mother who was saving your life through me."

There was a long silence. Then Robin said:

"I have hated everyone who put Mama in the ground. I wanted to kill them so that they would go in the ground too!"

"I am sure because you felt like that it made your mother very unhappy," Ila said, "but she would have understood that no one told you that she is watching over you and loving you, just as she did when she was on earth."

"But, why did she have to leave me?" Robin asked forlornly.

"I expect, if you think about it, you will know the answer to that," Ila replied.

"I suppose it was because she – wanted to be with – Papa."

"Of course she did," Ila said, "because they loved each other."

"But – they loved me too."

"They are still loving you and one day you will join them. But you have some very important work to do in the world before you can do so."

"Very important?" Robin enquired.

"But of course! You are a man, and every man has some special work which only he can do."

Robin thought for a moment.

"What do you think that work will be?"

Ila smiled.

"You will have to find that out for yourself. What is important is that whatever it is you have to be very, very good at it."

She saw that Robin understood and went on:

"You have to learn about it. The best way to do that is not only to have good teachers, but also to read, and read, and read!"

"Do you read books?" Robin asked.

"I read every moment I can," Ila said, "and it is so exciting. You can do such marvellous things by reading a book."

"What sort of things?"

"Climb mountains, dive down into the sea, see the Pyramids of Egypt, the Temples and Palaces of India. There are millions and millions of things we can do, just by opening a book!"

"Tell me which books," Robin begged.

Ila gave a little sigh.

"I . . I . . you must . . forgive me," she said, "but . . I feel suddenly . . very tired . . I think Nanny would . . want me to sleep . . We will . . go on . . talking about this . . when I . . wake up . . . ."

Her voice was fading away.

Robin got up from the chair in which he had been sitting.

"You go to sleep," he said, "and I will draw the curtains so that the sun will not keep you awake."

"Thank . . you . . . ." Ila said faintly.

The Marquis heard Robin move across the floor and quickly backed down the passage.

He was absolutely astounded by what he had heard.

He realised now that he and everybody else had handled Robin in the wrong way.

He could understand now the shock it had been to the small boy to lose his mother.

He blamed himself for not seeing that her death was properly explained to him.

Now at last he knew the reason why Robin had hated everybody and smashed things up.

He was rebelling, as far older people than he had, against Fate, which had taken away the person he loved.

Of course, the average Governess and also his relatives were not, he thought, particularly imaginative.

They had not understood the workings of his mind.

The Marquis had retreated almost to the kitchen when Robin came out of the bedroom.

He walked towards him saying:

"Good-morning, Robin."

"Hello, Uncle Osbert," Robin replied.

"I have brought you another pony which I would like you to see," the Marquis said. "You may think he is too big for you, but I would like you to consider riding him."

110

The Marquis knew as he spoke that he was offering his nephew a challenge.

He was therefore not surprised when Robin replied:

"I could ride a horse as big as yours!"

"I am sure you could," the Marquis answered, "but I would like you to try this pony first. His name is *Firefly*."

They walked out of the house as they were talking.

Robin saw *Firefly* with the groom standing beside him.

He was certainly a good deal bigger than *Rufus*, but the Marquis could not have thought of a better way of enticing Robin back on to a horse.

Robin walked up to *Firefly* and patted him.

The Marquis knew his father must have taught him to do that with a strange horse.

The groom helped him into the saddle.

"I think it would be a good idea," the Marquis said, "if you and I went riding alone. Then you can tell me what you think of *Firefly*."

"I would like that," Robin said.

"You wait here," the Marquis ordered the groom. "I am sure Mrs Wilcox will give you a cup of tea."

"Thank ye, M'Lord!" the groom replied.

The Marquis moved off and Robin followed him.

On the flat land he found, as he expected, that Robin could handle *Firefly* very well.

They rode for about an hour, and only as they returned did Robin say:

"Is this my pony now?"

"If you want him," the Marquis replied. "But I dare say you will soon be asking for something bigger. In the meantime, be careful with *Firefly*."

"I had better not take him into the wood where there are wasps' nests!" Robin said.

The Marquis was about to say that would be sensible, but instead replied:

"I do not want you to be worried about what happened

to *Rufus*. It is something that might happen once in a hundred years."

He saw that Robin was listening, and went on:

"In all the years I have been riding, and it is now something like twenty-six, I have never had any horse on which I have been riding, stung by a wasp."

"I think you are telling me that, Uncle Osbert, so that I am not frightened," Robin remarked.

"It is always a mistake to be nervous on a horse because they are very sensitive to one's reactions," the Marquis answered.

"Ila told me this morning that she loves her horse more than anything else in the world," Robin remarked.

"We will have to find you one that you will love," the Marquis said.

"I might love *Firefly*," Robin said and bent forward to pat his neck, "but I cannot know how much until I have ridden him many times."

"Of course," the Marquis agreed.

He thought, however, that Robin was far more intelligent than he had thought he was.

And if he was intelligent, he was undoubtedly sensitive.

"I must find someone who will teach him and also understand him," he told himself.

It was lunchtime when they got back to The House in the Wood.

The Marquis remembered he had not only to have luncheon, but also to call at the Castle.

He had almost forgotten he was to meet Lady Lavinia early this afternoon.

He therefore said goodbye to Robin and, without going into the house, rode back to Rake.

He had luncheon alone, then rode off to the Castle.

He was thinking as he did so how extraordinary it was that a perfect stranger and one as young and lovely as Ila should have understood Robin.

It was something no one else had been able to do.

She had already begun to change him from the problem child he had been up till now.

His mother would have been – or as Ila believed was – very proud.

"The whole thing seems extraordinary to me," he told himself.

At the same time, he thought that what had happened was a miracle.

As he neared the Castle it was with some difficulty that he brought his mind back to himself and his own problems.

Lady Lavinia would be waiting for him.

He had to propose marriage to her which was something he had never done before.

It was a very different thing to making love to one of the sophisticated, alluring Beauties.

They seduced him by every look, word and movement they made.

"If we have to live together for the rest of our lives," he thought rather gloomily, "then the sooner I can make her fall in love with me, the better!"

He did not think it would be very difficult.

Every woman he met was apparently overcome by his appearance and his charm.

Combined of course, he mused cynically, with the fact that he was the Marquis of Rakemoore.

"I am blessed with enough worldly goods to dazzle any young woman," he added to himself.

At the same time, although he was a reluctant bridegroom he must make sure she was not aware of it.

He had brought with him a diamond ring which he had taken out of the safe the night before.

Although it was not his mother's, it was a very impressive piece of jewellery.

He supposed when he put it on her finger he should kiss her.

He must also promise to do everything in his power to make her happy.

He could not help thinking how very much easier it could be. If she was one of the women who Nanny had called his 'Beautiful Ladies'.

Then there would be no problem.

She would be looking at him eagerly and ardently.

As their eyes met they would both be aware of a flame rising within them.

It would grow and grow until it became a consuming fire.

They would both be lost in the wild excitement of it.

Unfortunately as he well knew a fire dies down.

Where he was concerned there was all too often only the ashes – and the recriminations!

Yet with a young girl there would be no fire – only a sense of duty.

"Dammit all!" he said to himself. "I should have married a widow!"

The trouble was, he could not think of one who was available at the moment.

Anyway, he was now committed to the Duke's daughter, and there was nothing he could do about it.

He thought of the wedding which the Duke would undoubtedly be planning.

He would dislike it, however pretty his Bride might be.

He had attended too many weddings not to realise how superficial they were.

The interminable shaking of hands and the insincere, gushing good wishes would bore him.

He knew despairingly that he was bored with the whole farce.

All he wanted was to enjoy his life as he had previously, before the Queen's interference.

He tried to tell himself that actually he was very lucky.

If Peregrine had not been the nephew of the Lord Chamberlain he would, at this moment, have found himself at Windsor Castle.

He would be proposing marriage to the Princess Greta who would accept him in guttural English.

"I should be thankful for that at any rate," he said with a twist of his lips as he rode up to the front door of the Castle.

A groom was waiting to take his horse.

Only as he dismounted did it strike him that it would have been more appropriate if he had driven over correctly dressed.

After all it was his first proposal of marriage.

It was too late now.

He entered the Castle to find the Duke waiting for him in his Study.

"My dear boy, I am delighted to see you," the Duke said, "but I am afraid I have rather bad news!"

"Bad news?" the Marquis asked.

"I am afraid my dear little Lavinia has a very bad cold in the head, and a temperature, and it is therefore impossible for her to leave her bed today."

"That is very regrettable," the Marquis said.

"I would have sent a message over to tell you not to bother to join me," the Duke went on, "but I thought there was a great deal that we had to talk about."

"Yes, of course," the Marquis agreed.

He was thinking as he spoke that he had heard enough about the Duke's mares.

He must find an excuse to get away.

"I have been working out some figures for you . . ." the Duke began, "and I think if we use Trumpeter with . . ."

The Marquis stifled a yawn.

He had no idea of the effort the Duke was making to keep him amused.

It was only after breakfast this morning that His Grace had been informed that *Swallow* had returned yesterday.

"Why was I not told?" he demanded angrily.

Apparently none of the grooms had thought it unusual as Lady Lavinia often sent *Swallow* to the stables alone.

"Her Ladyship may have had an accident, you fools!" the Duke roared.

"The stirrups were lifted on to the pommel, Your Grace."

The Duke had to admit this would not have been done if Lavinia had fallen off.

Although he tried not to admit it he was beginning to believe that Lavinia really had run away.

"The silly little idiot does not realise what she is refusing," he kept thinking as he talked to the Marquis.

Ila did not wake until lunchtime.

Nanny brought her in a well-cooked dish of young chicken.

With it were new potatoes and very small peas fresh from the vegetable gardens at Rake.

When Ila finished her luncheon, she said:

"That was delicious! Thank you so much! I really feel much better and more like myself."

"Your head's not hurting you?" Nanny asked.

"It is just a little tender, but at the same time, I do not feel now as if my brain were stuffed with cotton wool."

"You'll soon be as right as rain," Nanny said, "and that's what we all want."

"I want you to come riding with me," Robin, who had just come into the bedroom, said. "I have a new pony and I want to show him to you."

"A new pony!" Ila exclaimed. "What is his name?"

"He is called *Firefly* and he is much bigger than *Rufus*."

116

"Then you will have to be very careful with him."

"That is what Uncle Osbert said when he took me riding with him this morning, and he went very, very fast."

"I am sure you are a good rider," Ila said, "and one day I will show you *Swallow*."

As she said her horse's name, she suddenly thought that perhaps it was a mistake.

If there was a hue and cry for Lady Lavinia Worth, some of those who lived near the Castle knew she always rode a horse called *Swallow*.

"That is a secret," she said to Robin. "I do not want you to talk about *Swallow* in case it makes the people who will be looking for me find me."

"Are they very bad and wicked?" Robin enquired.

"No, not really," Ila replied. "They just want me to do something which I know is wrong."

"And will you have to go on hiding from them for ever?" Robin enquired.

"I hope not," Ila replied, "but at least until they no longer try to make me do what I am determined not to do."

"You can hide here."

"That would be lovely for me," Ila replied, "but I think your Nanny might find it rather tiresome."

"She is not *my* Nanny!" Robin said. "She is Uncle Osbert's, and when he got too old for her to look after him he gave her this little house."

"What is your Uncle's name?" Ila asked.

Robin laughed.

"Of course, I forgot! You did not meet him! He came here and looked at you, but you were unconscious!"

"He looked at me?" Ila exclaimed. "You do not think he will talk about me?"

"No, of course not. I told him you were in hiding, and he said he would keep it a secret."

"I hope he does that," Ila said, "but you have not yet told me what your Uncle's name is."

"He is the Marquis of Rakemoore," Robin replied, "and lives in a big, big house called 'Rake'!"

Ila was still.

She felt as if her brain were once more full of cotton wool.

How was it possible that in saving Robin she had been brought to the house of the Marquis's Nanny?

For one moment it was impossible to speak and very difficult to think.

"I thought I hated Uncle Osbert," Robin was saying, "but today he was very nice to me, and we rode alone."

He smiled at her as he continued.

"When I have seen him before there have always been other people with him."

He was working it out for himself.

"When he came . . here and . . I was . . unconscious," Ila said, "did he . . say anything . . about me?"

"No," Robin answered, "and he did not come to see you this morning."

Ila gave a little sigh of relief.

At the same time, she knew that she would have to go away.

When the Marquis did come to see her again or rather, to see Robin, he would be certain to ask her questions.

It would be terrible if he guessed who she was.

"I must go away," she told herself.

The difficulty was she felt so weak.

When she got out of bed her head seemed to swim round.

"I will be all right tomorrow," she told herself optimistically.

She certainly felt better during the afternoon.

This was despite the fact that Robin was plying her with questions which she had some difficulty in answering.

In the end she told him a story.

It was one of the stories she had read of travelling through India.

The author had seen the Ganges, the Taj Mahal, then gone into Nepal to stay in the foothills of the Himalayas.

Because when she had first read it, she had lived it herself, she found it easy to describe to Robin the beauty, excitement and wonder of it.

Robin was sitting on her bed so that she did not have to raise her voice.

He was entranced by every word she spoke.

As she finished he said:

"Now I know what I am going to do when I grow up!"

"And what is that?" Ila enquired.

"I am going to be an Explorer," he said. "I will explore the world, and I will have one of those new cameras which Uncle Osbert has, and bring you back photographs of wherever I go."

Ila laughed.

"That would be lovely, and I will stick them all into an Album."

Robin's eyes lit up and she went on:

"You can write a book, and the photographs will be reproduced in it so that everybody will want to do what you have done."

Robin clapped his hands.

"In the meantime," Ila said, "you will have to start learning languages."

"Why?" Robin asked.

"It would be very frustrating to go to a country," Ila answered, "and not be able to understand when they are telling you about their Temples and all the other beautiful buildings."

"I will learn how to talk to them," Robin promised.

They talked about the places he would go to until finally Nanny came to shoo him out of Ila's bedroom.

"Our patient needs to rest, Master Robin," she said, "and you must not make her so tired that her head will ache."

"I would not want to do that!" Robin agreed.

He immediately jumped off the bed and said to Ila in an anxious voice:

"You are all right? I have not over-tired you, have I?"

Ila smiled at him.

"No, but I think I would like to sleep for a little while now before I have supper."

"Can I have supper with her?" Robin asked Nanny.

"If you carry in your own tray of food and put it on a small table by the bed, and move everything out afterwards," Nanny replied.

"I will do that."

"Then go out now and get some air." Nanny told him. "You'll find Mr Wilcox just outside in the wood. He's caught some small birds that have fallen out of their nest, and perhaps you could help him with them."

Robin gave a whoop of joy and ran off.

"He is the nicest little boy I have ever met!" Ila said.

"That's what I thinks," Nanny replied, "and all this nonsense about him being so naughty is just stupidity on the part of them as is supposed to be looking after him."

"What he needs," Ila said, "is somebody like you."

"If it comes to that," Nanny replied, "you're not doing so bad yourself!"

Ila laughed.

"Perhaps that is the sort of employment I ought to try and get," she said, "I never thought of it before."

"Well, think about it now," Nanny said. "It is like looking after animals. One either has a way with them, or one doesn't, and children are the same."

She took some of Ila's pillows away so that she could lie down and shutting out the sun, left her alone.

When she had gone, Ila thought over what they had just said.

"If there is a School in the village where I am hiding," she told herself, "I will see if I can teach in it, and if there is not, I must start a class of my own for little boys like Robin."

Then she fell asleep.

When Ila woke up and Nanny had pulled back the curtains she saw the sun was sinking in a blaze of glory.

"I'm going to give you your supper early," Nanny said. "Mr Wilcox likes his at six-thirty, and I can't be cooking two dinners at different times."

"No, of course not," Ila said, "and your food is so delicious that I am prepared to eat at any time it is convenient to you."

Robin came to tell her about the baby birds which he and Nanny's husband had, with great difficulty, put back in the nest.

"They were very hungry," he said, "and had their tiny beaks open."

"I expect that's what you are feeling," Nanny said. "So come along and get your tray, if you want to eat with Miss Ila."

"Of course I want to eat with her," Robin said. "I have been thinking about the lovely story she told me."

"No more stories tonight!" Nanny ordered. "You are both going to bed early, and no nonsense about it!"

She went from the room and Ila laughed.

"We have to do as Nanny says," she said, "and there is no use arguing."

"I like this Nanny," Robin said. "My last Nanny was horrid, and I cannot remember my first one."

"Well, think only of this Nanny, who is very special."

"She makes scrumptious food!" Robin remarked. "Far better than I get in the School-Room at Rake!"

"Do you have any meals with your Uncle?" Ila enquired.

Robin shook his head.

It was what she might have expected, she thought.

The Marquis was prepared to give his nephew a roof over his head, but not the love and attention the small boy needed.

'I am sure he is like Clementine's husband,' she told herself, 'pompous, and stuck up! He would not even be interested in his own children if he had them!'

She thought suddenly that if he had children they would also be hers. She felt herself shiver.

She was running away from a man who would not understand about any of the things that interested her.

How could he leave this poor little boy thinking his mother was buried in the ground and not explain that she was still near him and loving him?

Then she knew it was something she had not discussed with her own father.

She was also certain neither Phyllis nor Clementine could discuss it with their husbands.

"When I marry," she told herself, "it must be to a man who understands, otherwise I should only be miserable and unhappy and, wish I was dead!"

Nanny came to send Robin to bed, and helped Ila get ready to go to sleep.

"I expect when His Lordship comes to see Robin tomorrow," she said, "he'll want to meet you. He was here this morning, but I understand he didn't see you."

"Did Robin tell you that?" Ila asked.

"Yes, and his Uncle took him riding and when he brought Robin back here, he rode straight on to Rake."

Ila was silent for a moment. Then she said;

"The Marquis, I understand, is somebody who is very important."

"Very important indeed," Nanny agreed. "And who

can blame him for being pleased with himself about it? Although, as I tells him often enough, it's bad for him to have everything he wants in the world!''

Everything but me! Ila added silently.

Chapter Six

Ila crept on tiptoe down the corridor to the front door.

She had got out of bed hoping she would feel strong enough to run away.

She had slept well.

It was a great relief to find that her head was clear and her feet were steady.

Everything she possessed had been put by Nanny in a wardrobe and a chest of drawers.

She packed them in her white shawl and put on her riding habit.

When she dressed she felt she could not go away without an explanation.

There was a piece of paper on the table.

She had drawn for Robin a picture of a Pyramid, a Mosque and a very high mountain.

The back was blank, and she wrote on it:

"*Dear Nanny,*
Thank you so very much for being so kind to me. I have to go on my way, but please tell Robin that I shall be thinking of him, and praying for him.

I have been very happy in your pretty house. Thank you again.

Love,
Ila"

She left the letter on her pillow before she opened the door very carefully so that it would not make a noise.

Now she did the same with the front door which fortunately had a well-oiled lock.

Then she was out in the wood.

She moved quickly between the trees, and along the path where Robin had been riding when she first saw him.

She was aware he would be upset that she had gone away.

There was nothing she could do if she encountered the Marquis.

"I must not meet him," she told herself. "If I do, he might guess who I am."

She thought of several ways that he could do so.

If her father had described the colour of her hair.

If he had seen a portrait of her mother at the Castle whom she resembled.

The mere fact that Lady Lavinia Worth was missing might make him suspicious.

She reached the end of the path, and the cliff made by the landslide was just ahead.

She, however, turned right to find the path which would take her down into the valley.

She knew it went to the two villages, one of which she was certain was where Miss Dunkill lived.

She had casually asked Nanny their names when she was helping her into bed last night.

"One is called Bantry," Nanny replied, "which is the biggest of the two, and the other, which's nearer, is Fording-Field."

The last name sounded familiar to Ila.

She felt certain this was where she would find Miss Dunkill.

"At least I can ask for her and if she is not there, I can walk on to somewhere else," she told herself.

Because the path was rough, stony, and it was easy to slip, it took her a long time to reach the ground below.

She was a little tired because it was the first exercise she had taken since she had hit her head.

She sat down under a tree.

It was very quiet and the rising sun cast a golden glow over the land.

Ila found herself thinking of Robin and how upset he would be when he found she was missing.

It is unkind of me to leave him, she thought, but what else can I do?

Once again she could see her sisters' pale, strained faces.

She could hear the despair in Phyllis's voice when she told her how unhappy she was.

"How could I get like that?" she asked herself. "I would rather be dead!"

At the same time, because the world was beautiful, she wanted to live.

She wanted to ride *Swallow* in the woods.

She wanted to dream of one day finding a man she loved and who would love her.

They would have a son like Robin and other children who would never be neglected or unhappy.

"How can I marry somebody like the Marquis?" she asked, "and know that he would never understand what I was thinking and dreaming?"

She sighed and added, "He would neglect our children, as he has neglected Robin."

Because she was frightened that the Marquis might look for her as her father was doing, she jumped to her feet.

She set off in the direction of Fording-Field.

It was a small village with little thatched cottages and an ancient Norman Church.

There was also a row of Alms Houses which she thought looked quite attractive.

There were two shops.

Already women with shawls over their heads and baskets on their arms were going into one.

It was obviously the Grocer's.

Ila thought that if she went in amongst them she would, because she was a stranger, cause too much curiosity.

She walked on a little further.

Now the cottages were further apart, and had small gardens that were bright with flowers.

She was wondering if she should knock on the door of one of them and ask if they knew Miss Dunkill.

Then an elderly woman with a kind face came walking towards her.

She carried an empty basket on her arm, and Ila knew she was going to the Grocer's.

As she reached her she said:

"Excuse me, but could you tell me if there is an old lady in this village called Miss Dunkill?"

The woman stared at her.

"Ye be askin' for Miss Dunkill?" she said as if she felt she could not have heard aright.

"Yes, I am," Ila replied.

"Then I am sure ye're one of 'er relatives," the woman said. "I says one o'em would turn up sooner or later!"

She saw that Ila looked puzzled and went on:

"I'm sorry but I've bad news for ye. Miss Dunkill – God rest 'er soul – were buried three days ago."

"Buried?" Ila repeated stupidly. "Then she is dead!"

"I'm afraid so," the woman said. "'Twas a peaceful end an' her didn't suffer."

"I'm glad about that," Ila said, "but I had hoped to see her."

"I'm sure ye did, dear, an' it's a real shame ye're too late."

Ila did not speak, wondering what she should do next, and the woman went on:

"Now I'm sure ye want t' go t' 'er cottage, an' I expects as ye're her relative it'll now be yours."

Ila looked surprised.

"Mine?" she murmured not understanding.

"Yes, yours, dear, 'less another relative 'as more claim. Now come along wi' me, an' I'll show ye where 'tis."

She turned back the way she had come, and Ila walked beside her.

"I expect ye knows Miss Dunkill inherited th' cottage from 'er brother an' very happy 'er was there."

Ila thought the less said the better.

She therefore merely made a sound of being interested.

Then the woman went on:

"Everyone in th' village were fond of 'er, an' I suppose nearly everyone took their troubles to 'er at one time or another. We'll miss 'er, that we shall!"

She was still talking when they reached the pretty thatched cottage which was at the very end of the village.

The garden was well kept and had a flagged path leading up to the front door.

The woman walked ahead and put up her hand to take the key from the lintel.

She put it in the lock, opened the door and went in.

Ila followed her.

She saw a small, spotlessly clean room which was comfortably furnished.

It was the kitchen but there were rugs on the floor.

She could see carpet on the floor of the room on the other side which she knew must be the Parlour.

"Ye'll find everything spick an' span," her guide was saying. "We always used t' laugh and say there were never a speck o' dust in Miss Dunkill's cottage an' no mouse dare put 'is nose inside th' wainscotting!"

She laughed at her own joke.

"You are very kind to show it to me," Ila said. "May I ask your name?"

"It's Mrs Cosnett, dear. Me husband's the Postman an' very busy it keeps him, though ye wouldn't think so in such a small place."

Ila looked round the cottage.

"I would love to stay here," she said.

"I'm sure we'd all love to 'ave ye," Mrs Cosnett replied. "We was half-afraid we'd get someone we knew nothing about in th' village, an' we likes to keep ourselves to ourselves!"

She spoke so positively that Ila could not help smiling.

She knew in the village nearest the Castle they looked on strangers as if they were foreigners.

"Now, if ye're setting up house," Mrs Cosnett said, "I 'spect ye'll want somethin' to eat, though I dare say ye'll find there's tea in th' cupboard."

She opened a kitchen cupboard which seemed to be filled with pots.

Some of them were labelled in neat hand-writing which was obviously Miss Dunkill's.

Mrs Cosnett was reading the labels.

"Now let me see – ah! Here's th' tea, there's at least half a pound for ye. But ye'll need some milk, an' I expect, a loaf of fresh bread."

"Can I get all that from the Grocer's?" Ila asked.

She suddenly felt a little tired, and sat down in a chair.

"Where have you come from?" Mrs Cosnett asked.

"I walked down the path near the landslide," Ila replied.

"Oh, that was terrible, that was!" Mrs Cosnett said. "The rumble an' fall of it frightened the life out o' me."

"I am sure it did!"

"It's dangerous – that's what it is!" Mrs Cosnett went on. "I hear a pony fell down it th' day afore yesterday. Killed th' poor creature, it did! There should be a fence on th' top!"

She did not wait for Ila to make a comment, but continued:

"Ye do look tired! I'll make ye a cup o' tea, then I'll tell ye what I'll do. I'll go to th' shop an' send one of th' boys back with yer orders. It'll save your feet 'til ye're rested."

"That is very kind of you, very kind indeed," Ila said. "I am most grateful."

"You'll find everyone in Fording-Field will do anything for one o' Miss Dunkill's relatives," Mrs Cosnett said, "an' as you're so pretty, dear, th' men'll do any repairs ye need t' the cottage, just as they did for yer . . ."

She paused.

"What relation were Miss Dunkill to ye?"

Ila thought quickly.

"She . . she was . . my great Aunt," she answered.

"That's what I thought her must be!" Mrs Cosnett exclaimed.

While she was talking she had lit the stove which had been already laid.

In less than five minutes she had the kettle boiling.

She poured the hot water into a brown teapot in which she had previously put a large spoonful of tea.

"Ye'll have to drink it wi'out milk 'til I can send ye some," she said, "but it'll at least 'wet yer whistle', as me father used t' say."

She laughed, and as if she thought Ila looked surprised explained:

"He were a sailor when 'e were young, an' always used a nautical expression if 'e could."

"If you are going to the shops," Ila said, "may I give you the money for the things I require?"

"There's no hurry for that," Mrs Cosnett answered. "Th' boy as brings ye th' goods'll leave ye a bill which ye can pay when ye feel like walking down t' Mr Johnson's."

She laughed again as she said:

"I can tell you one thing: they'll all be wantin' to see ye an' it's a 'feather in me cap' that I've got in first!"

As if it struck her that as soon as she reached the Grocer's she could announce her discovery, she moved towards the door.

"Now ye make yerself at home, dearie," she said, "and as ye look a bit peeky, I'd 'ave a lie down."

That in fact was what Ila wanted to do.

She found there were two bedrooms up some very narrow stairs.

Someone from the village must have tidied up after Miss Dunkill died and put clean sheets on both the beds.

She wished she could remember more about her old Governess.

But nothing could be more fortunate than that she could step into a place where her father would not find her.

'How could he imagine for one moment I would be in a village?' she thought. 'He will expect me to go to one of my friends.'

A young boy, as Mrs Cosnett had promised, brought her a basket containing everything she required.

There were eggs, potatoes, bacon, sausages and a newly-baked cottage loaf as well as a large pat of butter.

There was also a pint of milk and what she thought very touching, a comb of honey from the village Beekeeper.

"'E sez," the small boy explained, "that as Miss Dunkill were – ever so kind when e' were ill – 'e's sent this to – welcome ye to – Fording-Field."

He said all this in a quick, rather breathless fashion.

It told Ila he was trying to remember what he had been told to say.

"Will you please thank the gentleman, very, very much," she said, "and tell him I hope to meet him once I am settled in."

"Oi'll tell 'e, Miss," the boy said as he turned to go.

As he did so she put a three-penny bit in his hand with which he was delighted.

"Thank ye, Miss, thank ye!" he said. "Oi've bin wantin' to buy a toffee-apple!"

He went off quickly as if afraid she would change her mind and want the three pence back.

It made her think of Robin.

She wished she could give him a toffee-apple and go on explaining to him what books he should read.

"I should have brought him with me," she thought.

Then she knew that would have been a very dangerous thing to do.

She cooked two of the eggs and a little bacon for her luncheon.

Then she climbed up the narrow, twisting stairs.

Both the bedrooms had sloping ceilings and she thought it would be impossible for a tall man to stand up in them.

All she wanted to do at the moment, however, was to rest.

As soon as she lay down she fell fast asleep.

If anybody knocked on the door hoping to see her, she would not have heard them.

Ila awoke to find it was late in the afternoon.

Looking through the window she saw that the shadows of the trees were growing long and the sun was sinking behind them.

"I must find out if there is any way to light the cottage," she told herself.

She went down the stairs, stoked up the stove and put the kettle on to make a cup of tea.

Then she found to her relief there were two oil lamps.

One was in a corner of the kitchen she had not noticed before.

They were both half full and their wicks looked comparatively new.

She discovered in a drawer a box of candles which would light her way to the bedroom.

Otherwise she would have to carry up one of the oil lamps when she went to bed.

Miss Dunkill had obviously made herself very comfortable.

The elegant antimacassars on the chairs, and the embroidered cushions told Ila how she had occupied herself in her old age.

"Thank You, thank You, God for letting me come here," she said in her heart.

She started as there was a knock on the door.

She walked across the kitchen to open it.

Outside, to her astonishment, she saw Robin.

He gave a shrill cry and flung himself against her.

"I have . . found you! I have . . found you!" he cried.

Because he was reaching up to put his arms around her neck, Ila went down on her knees.

He put his cheek against hers and held her so tightly that she could hardly breathe.

"I thought – I had lost – you," he said, "and I walked and – walked!"

Then he burst into tears.

Now Ila was holding him as close as he was holding her, and murmuring:

"It is all right, darling . . it is all right, you have found me. But how could you have come all this way . . by yourself?"

Robin was incapable of answering her and she picked him up in her arms.

She took him inside the kitchen.

There was a comfortable armchair in which she sat down and took him on her lap.

For a minute or two he just cried and she could only say:

"I am here and you have been very . . very . . brave."

At the same time she was wondering frantically what would happen when the Marquis heard that Robin was missing.

"I – I could not – lose you," Robin was saying through his tears. "I – looked – for you in the – wood . . ."

"And now you have found me," Ila said, "and you must have some supper as I am sure you are very hungry!"

"You are – quite – safe?" Robin asked, raising his face so that he could look at her.

"I am safe here in this dear little cottage," Ila said, "but I am very worried that you should have come after me. Nanny will be very anxious."

"I told her I had to find you," Robin said, "and after I had looked and looked in the woods – I came down a path into another village."

"That must have been Bantry," Ila said.

"I asked if they had seen a pretty lady with golden hair, and they laughed at me, so I came to this village."

He paused to catch his breath before he went on:

"A boy told me there was someone new in the cottage at the end of the village."

"So that is how you found me!" Ila said. "Well, you were very clever! Now, suppose you wash your hands and help me cook something delicious to eat?"

As she spoke she wiped the tears from Robin's cheeks.

She felt like crying herself because he had been so determined to find her.

She knew it must have been a frightening experience for a small boy when he did not even know her proper name.

Obediently, Robin went into the scullery at the back of the kitchen.

Ila poured some hot water out of the kettle into the basin that was in the sink.

While Robin was washing she went back into the kitchen.

134

There was still some bacon left, the sausages which she had not touched, and four eggs.

She cooked them all, and toasted some slices of bread.

When Robin came to join her his tears were all gone and he said excitedly:

"That smells scrumptious, and my tummy is very empty!"

"I am sure it is," Ila said. "Sit down at the table. There is plenty of food to fill it."

He ate a very good meal.

She realised how hungry he had been, having had nothing since breakfast.

While they were eating he told her how Nanny had thought her to be asleep.

She therefore did not go into her bedroom until they had finished their breakfast.

"Then I suppose, she found my note," Ila said.

"Nanny found it and said: 'She's gone away, and she's not well enough to go off on her own!'"

Robin ate a large mouthful of sausage before he went on:

"It was then I thought perhaps you had gone in the wood and I ran off to look and look – but there was no sign of you."

"Nanny will be very worried when you do not go back," Ila said.

"I am not going back," Robin replied. "I am going to stay with you and look after you. If you are alone in the cottage you will need somebody to protect you."

Ila smiled.

"It would be lovely to have you do that," she answered, "but I think perhaps your Uncle will be looking for you."

"He will not expect to find me here," Robin said.

Ila thought that was the truth.

But she knew it was impossible for her to keep Robin. The Marquis would be determined to find him.

Perhaps he would be more effective at doing so than her father had been in finding her.

She was trying to think of an answer to the problem.

She knew Robin would not want to return without her.

"What shall I do?" she asked herself.

She did not say anything to Robin, she merely let him enjoy his supper.

When he had finished she knew that he was very tired.

He had been walking all day, first in the wood.

She calculated he must have spent several hours there before it struck him that she had gone down the hill into the village.

Of course he was tired.

Besides being anxious and afraid, although he would not have admitted it, both would have taken their toll.

"I have been sleeping all the afternoon," she said, "but even so, I am going to go to bed early."

"I am staying here with you," Robin said with an aggressive note in his voice.

"Of course you are!" Ila replied, "and fortunately, there is a very comfortable bedroom for you next to mine. It is on the left at the top of the stairs."

She smiled as she said:

"I am afraid I have not a nightshirt for you, so you will have to undress and sleep as you are."

"I do not mind that," Robin said, "and you will sleep next door?"

"I am coming to bed as soon as I have washed up the dishes," Ila said, "and I will come in and say good-night to you."

"That will be nice," Robin answered.

He ran up the stairs and Ila took the dishes into the scullery and washed them.

By this time it was dusk outside, and she lit one of the oil lamps and put it on the kitchen table.

136

She thought now that she would take it up to her bedroom.

First though, she would provide Robin with a candle in case he should wake in the night and feel afraid.

She found a candlestick with a handle on the dresser, and put a new candle into it.

Then, having lit it with a spill from the fire, she walked up the stairs.

Robin was waiting for her, looking small and vulnerable.

She set the candle down beside him and sat down on the mattress.

"First of all," she said, "I want to thank you for thinking of me and being so kind as to come all this way so that you could look after me."

"Nanny said you were too pretty to be left all by yourself," Robin said, "and I think you are very pretty!"

"Thank you, Robin," Ila replied. "That is the nicest compliment I have ever been paid."

She took his hand in hers.

"Now," she said, "I am going to thank God in my prayers that you got here safely, and I know it was your mother who told you how to find me."

"I talked to her as you told me to," Robin said, "and she said to me: 'Ask for a pretty girl with golden hair!' "

Ila laughed.

"That is a nice thing to say. At the same time, it was very intelligent of you."

She put her arms around the little boy and kissed him.

She knew as she did so that it was what he had been missing since his mother had died.

He held on to her very tightly.

"You will – not run – away in the – night?" he asked in a small voice.

"No, of course not," Ila said. "I shall be here in the morning, just across the passage from you."

"Will you tell me a story tomorrow?"

"Of course I will," Ila answered. "But I expect there will be lots of things to do. We have to explore the cottage, and of course, the village."

"That will be fun!" Robin said.

She kissed him again and felt him kiss her in return.

She opened the door before she blew out the candle.

"God bless you!" she said as her mother had always said to her. "And may the Angels watch over you."

Closing the door Ila went down the stairs to fetch the oil lamp.

She was just lifting it off the table when there was a knock on the front door.

She wondered if it were Mrs Cosnett.

She could not think it would be anybody else so late, although she supposed it was not much after seven o' clock.

She opened the door.

Outside there was a man.

As she moved a trifle, the light from the lamp shone on his face and she felt her heart miss a beat.

There was no need for anyone to tell her who it was.

The smart riding-clothes, the shining boots and the top-hat set a little on one side of his dark hair could only belong to one person.

She stared at him, finding it impossible to think or breathe.

Suddenly she realised he did not look in the least as she had expected.

He was younger, better-looking, in fact the most handsome man she had ever seen.

There seemed to be an interminable silence until the Marquis asked:

"May I come in?"

"Y . . yes . . yes . . of . . course!" Ila stammered.

She stood to one side as he entered the cottage.

138

In the kitchen he seemed larger and more over-whelming than he had on the doorstep.

Then, as if she came back to reality, Ila said:

"R.Robin is . . here . . he is quite . . safe."

"I thought that this was where he would be!" the Marquis answered. "But, of course, I have been worried about him."

"I . . I am . . sorry," Ila said. "I never . . thought he would . . follow me."

The Marquis looked at her.

She had moved to the other side of the table.

Because she was frightened her eyes seemed to fill her whole small pointed face.

He thought they were the most amazing eyes he had ever seen in his whole life.

Her golden hair glowed against the white walls.

She seemed insubstantial.

It was not surprising he thought that at one moment this afternoon he thought she had vanished into the pool in the wood never to be found again.

"May I sit down?" he asked after what seemed a long pause.

"I . . I am . . sorry . . I should have . . asked you to do so," Ila said, "b . . but . . it was such a . . surprise . . seeing you."

"It has taken me quite a long time," the Marquis admitted.

"H.how . . how did you . . find me?"

The Marquis settled himself comfortably in what was an upright chair.

But Miss Dunkill had padded the seat and covered it in a red material.

"It was Nanny," he repled. "She thought you might have gone to one of the villages, so I came first to Fording-Field."

"And . . you thought . . Robin would be . . with me?"

"As he was several hours in advance of me, I hoped that if he failed to find you he would come back to Nanny."

"It was . . very brave of him to . . search for . . me as he did. He only found me . . a little over an . . hour ago, and he is very . . tired."

"So you have put him to bed," the Marquis said.

"I was just on my way to bed, too."

He gave a little laugh.

"If you only knew the commotion you have both caused as far as I am concerned! I was terrified of what might have happened to Robin and also to you."

Ila looked away from him.

"I am . . not really . . your concern."

"That is not true," the Marquis replied. "You saved my nephew's life, for which I owe you a debt of gratitude, and made yourself important to Nanny, who was almost in tears when I left her."

He paused, and as Ila did not speak, he went on:

"You are also very important to Robin, or he would not have run after you the way he did. He might have got into serious trouble, if he had been unable to find you."

"I . . I am . . sorry," Ila said again in a very small voice. "I am . . very . . sorry that I . . should have . . upset everybody . . so much."

"I feel it is what you will do wherever you go," the Marquis remarked.

Ila did not know whether he meant it as a compliment or a rebuke, and blushed.

"You are very beautiful, Ila!" the Marquis said quietly. "Do you really intend to live alone in this cottage – and does it actually belong to you?"

Ila was just going to tell him that it had belonged to her old Governess.

Then she thought it would be a mistake.

"I see . . no reason why . . I should not . . stay here," she replied, "at least . . for a little . . while."

"No reason?" the Marquis repeated. "You are being evasive, but you must realise that looking as you do and being what Nanny calls a 'Lady', it is impossible for you to live alone."

"I am sure I shall be quite safe in Fording-Field," Ila said defiantly.

"You might, and you might not," the Marquis said after a pause, "but of course, there is also the problem of Robin."

Ila did not know what to answer.

Then as he was obviously waiting for her to say something she said:

"Perhaps . . he could . . stay with me . . for a little . . while?"

"I doubt if he would be content with that," the Marquis said, "and I am afraid you will have not only the whole village talking about you, but a number of people in the County."

Ila clasped her hands together.

"You . . you know . . I am . . in hiding?"

"We are all aware of that!" the Marquis answered with a smile. "However, it is going to be difficult for you to go on doing so."

"Then . . I suppose I shall have to find . . somewhere else," Ila said.

The Marquis bent towards her.

"Would it not be much easier if you trusted me?" he asked. "I am supposed to be a rather intelligent man when there are difficulties and problems, and I feel sure I could help solve yours."

Ila shook her head.

"No . . that is . . something you . . could never . . do!"

The Marquis raised his eyebrows.

"You seem very positive about that! Suppose you tell me . . ."

Ila got to her feet.

"No . . no! It is impossible . . absolutely impossible!"

She walked across the room as if she was searching for a way to escape from him.

The Marquis watched her.

He was thinking that no one could look more lovely.

It was a beauty he had never seen before and which, like the colour of her hair, was completely unique.

Then as if she wanted to change the subject, Ila said:

"You have . . not yet told me how you . . found me when you . . did not even . . know my name."

The Marquis gave a little laugh.

"Once I reached Fording-Field, it was quite easy," he answered. "I called on the Vicar who told me that a relative of one of the oldest and most respected inhabitants who had recently died, had just arrived to take over her cottage."

"It was as easy as that!" Ila exclaimed.

"Then, just as I was leaving the Vicarage," the Marquis went on, "the Vicar's wife came in to say that she had heard from their servant that a small boy had also arrived in the village and had joined the young woman in Miss Dunkill's cottage."

"It is not fair!" Ila cried. "When poor Robin spent all day trying to find me!"

"But he succeeded!" the Marquis said. "And as it is the first time he has cared for anybody since his mother died, he would have gone on searching, however long it took to find you!"

Ila felt tears come into her eyes.

"I love him," she said, "but what can . . I do?"

She spoke weakly, thinking it impossible for anybody to understand the predicament she was in.

142

"I have a solution to that," the Marquis said. "I have just thought of it!"

"What . . is it?" Ila asked.

"You can stay here for a day or two, although it may cause comment you would wish to avoid," he said. "Then you must become Robin's official Governess and look after him."

Ila stared at him.

It was something that had never entered her mind.

She thought frantically that he was making things even more complicated than they were already.

As if the Marquis could read her thoughts, he said:

"I feel you will not want to go to Rake, but I have a great number of of other houses."

"You mean . . I could go to . . one of them . . with Robin?"

Ila spoke very slowly as if she was trying to convince herself that this was not a dream.

It seemed incredible that the very man from whom she had been running away should now be offering her a position of employment.

He was also trying to protect her from the gossip there would be if it was known she had run away from him.

"Unless you wish to break Robin's heart, and I never knew until now that he had one!" the Marquis said. "I think it is the best possible solution for him, and also perhaps the sanctuary you are seeking for yourself."

Ila sat down in a chair as if her legs would no longer support her.

"I have . . to think . . about . . this!" she gasped.

"Of course you must."

The Marquis got to his feet.

"What I am going to do, Ila," he said, "is to ride home knowing that both you and Robin are quite safe until tomorrow."

He hesitated, then said:

"But you will have to promise me by everything you hold Holy that you will not run away again first thing in the morning."

"I . . promise I will . . not do that," Ila said.

"Very well then, I will return to Rake and tomorrow, you and I will talk and decide where you would like to go."

He smiled.

"You really have a very large choice, including if you want woods, I have a house in the New Forest."

"I . . I do not know . . what to say," Ila said.

"Then sleep on it," the Marquis said. "I will come back tomorrow and bring Robin some clothes, and I am certain wherever you go, the two of you will both want horses to ride."

"H.how did you . . know I love riding?" Ila asked.

"I am sure you ride extremely well," he answered, "although perhaps, if you really are a nymph from the pool in the wood as I thought when I heard you had disappeared, you prefer swimming!"

Ila stared at him.

How could he possibly talk about the nymphs which she had always believed existed in the centre of the wood?

The Marquis turned towards the door.

"I am trusting you to keep your promise," he said, "otherwise, I feel, to make quite certain neither of you run away, I shall have to spend the night on the sofa in the Parlour."

Ila laughed because it sounded so funny.

"We will be . . here in the . . morning . . My Lord."

The Marquis opened the door.

Then he looked back.

"Good-night, Ila," he said. "Sleep well!"

He walked out, shutting the door behind him.

Because she could not help herself she ran to the window.

144

The Marquis was whistling for his horse which was cropping grass on the rough land that lay just beyond the cottage.

She knew it was *Saracen*, which Robin had told her was a most exceptional stallion.

The horse obeyed the Marquis' summons and he mounted him.

Then as if he was aware that Ila was watching him leave from the window, he swept off his hat.

As he rode away, she thought that no man could look so magnificent and so much a part of the big black stallion he was riding.

As he vanished into the darkness she told herself he was different.

Different in every way from what she had expected.

Chapter Seven

The Marquis found it difficult to sleep.

He tossed and turned and found himself going over and over the problem of Ila.

How could she stay with Robin and at the same time hide?

He tried to think of what it was that was making her so frightened.

When she had come to the door of the cottage and had seen him, there was a fear he had never seen in a woman's eyes before.

"What can be making her so afraid?" he asked himself, and turned over again.

Finally, soon after dawn, he rang for his Valet.

"You're early this morning, M'Lord!"

"I have a lot to do," the Marquis replied.

"We're not goin' back t' London, M'Lord?"

"No!"

It was a brief monosyllable, and spoken so positively that the Valet did not ask any more questions.

The Marquis ordered *Saracen* to be brought to the front of the house.

When he went downstairs he refused a suggestion from the footman on duty that he might want breakfast.

He had already decided he would have breakfast with Ila and Robin.

At the back of his mind he was almost obsessed with

the idea that despite her promise to him, she would run away.

"For some reason she wished to leave the vicinity," he told himself, "and she expects I will be coming over later in the day."

It was only six o'clock when he left Rake and galloped his horse over the fields towards the wood.

He could have gone by another route to Fording-Field.

But he wanted for some reason he did not wish to explain to himself, to go through the wood.

When he reached the pool in the centre he stopped.

He looked into it, again refusing to admit his reason for doing so.

It was not yet seven o'clock when he rode into the village.

He realised because there were two women hurrying down the main street that they were going to the shops.

It was then he thought that if he asked Ila for breakfast, it would be doubtful if she would have anything in the cottage.

He reasoned it out.

Robin had arrived unexpectedly and as she had given him supper, there would therefore be very little left for breakfast.

He stopped at the Grocer's shop and went inside.

There were only two elderly women at the counter.

They moved aside to stare at him in astonishment.

"Good morning!" the Marquis said to the man who was serving. "I need some food with which I am sure you can supply me."

"Certainly, M'Lord, an' it's an honour to 'ave Your Lordship here!"

The Marquis smiled.

"You know who I am?"

"Of course, M'Lord! We all remembers 'ow you comes

down to open the Alms Houses nigh on six year ago, an' we saw ye after the landslide."

"Yes, yes, of course," the Marquis said. "It is nice to see you again."

He held out his hand and the Grocer shook it.

"Now, what I 'spects Your Lordship requires is some- thin' for the Lady and the young gent'man in Miss Dunkill's cottage."

"The boy is my nephew," the Marquis explained, "and he spent the night there with his Governess."

He realised that the old women in the shop were list- ening to every word.

He thought, if nothing else, he had protected Ila's reputation.

He was well aware what they would suspect if he were visiting somebody as pretty as she was.

Mr Johnson was piling a whole variety of goods into a basket.

As he added a loaf of bread he said:

"I hopes that's everything ye'll want, M'Lord, an' I'll send th' boy with it immediate."

"That is very kind of you," the Marquis replied, "and do not forget some milk, which I am sure my nephew drinks."

He hesitated, then asked:

"Shall I settle the account now?"

"Ah, no, M'Lord! The boy'll bring it to ye," Mr Johnson said. "An' there's a small amount owin' from yesterday."

"Send both accounts to me at the cottage," the Marquis ordered. "Good day to you!"

He raised his hat to the two women.

They were staring at him with expressions of excitement and admiration on their faces.

He walked out of the shop and swung himself back into *Saracen*'s saddle.

148

He rode to the end of the road.

It was still not quite seven o'clock, and he wondered if Ila was asleep.

He knocked on the door and it was opened almost immediately.

Ila looked at him and as their eyes met, it was what had happened last night.

They stared at each other, and it was difficult to look away.

"You are . . early!" Ila exclaimed at length.

"I have come to breakfast," the Marquis replied.

She moved to allow him to enter the kitchen and as he did so she said:

"If you have had no breakfast you must be hungry, but . . I have nothing to give you. We ate it all last night."

"I am a practical man," the Marquis smiled, "and our breakfast is on its way."

He was looking at her as he spoke.

When Ila had got up she had put on one of the gowns she had brought with her because it was very light in weight.

The soft muslin clung to her figure.

Because it was green it made her look more like a nymph than usual.

Because she had not expected the Marquis so early she had left her hair hanging down her back.

She had just tied it at the nape of her neck with a green ribbon.

She looked, the Marquis thought, like Spring itself.

Or rather, as if she belonged to the woods, was part of them and not really human.

Because he was staring at her she said in an embarrassed tone:

"I apologise for not yet having arranged my hair . . but I did not expect . . visitors . . and I . . wanted to get . .

the stove going so that . . when Robin waked . . I could go . . to the shop and buy . . some eggs."

"I expect he is very tired after his adventures of yesterday," the Marquis remarked.

"He was half-asleep as I kissed him good-night!"

"He let you kiss him?" the Marquis asked.

"He kissed me when he found me," Ila said, "and I thought what he has been missing since his mother died is someone to . . love him."

"Of course that is what he wants," the Marquis agreed.

There was a knock on the door.

Before Ila could do so, the Marquis opened it.

It was the same boy who had delivered her goods yesterday and to whom she had given threepence.

"'Ere be yer order, M'Lord," he said, "and t'milk's in the can!"

The Marquis took both the basket and the can from him and put them down on the kitchen table.

Ila saw the boy was waiting expectantly.

"I gave him threepence yesterday," she said in a whisper.

The Marquis' eyes twinkled as he said:

"Then I think we might afford to double it today."

He gave the boy a sixpenny piece and he took it too excitedly to know what to say.

The Marquis shut the door.

"I hope there is everything you want," he said, "because I am hungry, and I am sure Robin will be when he comes downstairs."

"If we talk quietly," Ila said, "we will not waken him. I am sure he should have a long sleep after all he went through."

"It is what I needed too," the Marquis said. "But I kept waking up because I was afraid you would break your promise and run away again."

Ila looked at him in surprise.

150

"I would not . . have done that . . it would have been . . wrong."

"How could I be sure?" the Marquis asked. "Coming through the woods just now I stopped at the pool, just in case I should find you at the bottom of it!"

Ila stared at him.

It seemed so strange that he should have a pool in his wood, just as her father had one in his.

It was even stranger that he should connect her with it, when it meant so much to her.

This was something she was afraid of in a different way than she had been before.

She bent over the basket, looking to see what was in it.

Without speaking, she took out its contents, one by one, and put them on dishes by the stove.

There were eggs, sausages, bacon, just as there had been yesterday, but in larger amounts.

"Would you prefer coffee, or tea?" she asked the Marquis.

She had found a pot of coffee in the cupboard.

"I really do not mind," the Marquis replied. "Whatever you are making."

He spoke vaguely, as if he were thinking of something else.

He had put his hat down just inside the door when he entered the cottage.

Now he was sitting in the same chair in which he had sat last night.

He watched Ila as she moved backwards and forwards from the table to the stove.

There was a long silence.

At length he said:

"I can see you are an experienced cook."

"My mother thought it important that my sisters and I should all learn how to cook well."

"Then you have sisters!" the Marquis remarked quietly. "When are you going to tell me who you are, Ila?"

Realising she had made a mistake, she did not answer.

"I was thinking last night when I could not sleep," the Marquis went on, "of my houses where you might take Robin. Then I came to the conclusion that the whole idea was actually completely impracticable."

Ila turned from the stove to look at him.

"Why should you say that?" she asked.

It was something she had thought herself, but because he was saying it she was frightened.

It flashed through her mind that he no longer wanted her to teach Robin.

But she knew if she were separated from the small boy, he would be as frantic as he had been yesterday.

He would try to follow her, wherever she went.

It was all a jumble in her mind.

But she wanted to know the answer to what he had just said.

The Marquis hesitated as if feeling for words.

Then he said:

"You are too beautiful, and wherever you go, people will notice you, talk about you, and also if you are resident in one of my houses, it would undoubtedly be misconstrued."

It took Ila a few seconds to understand the meaning behind the words.

She blushed and turned away from him.

"I think," the Marquis went on, "that it would be much more sensible if you told me why you are running away, and what you intend to do in the future."

He was thinking that as she was a Lady, perhaps he could persuade one of his relatives to take her on as a companion.

Or even chaperon her in some place where she would

not be connected with the people from whom she was hiding.

When she did not speak he said:

"We have to discuss this, Ila!"

"There is . . no reason why I . . should do so . . with you!"

"That is an unkind remark when I am trying to help you!"

"But . . you cannot . . help me."

"And you cannot leave Robin."

"Perhaps . . I shall . . have to."

"How can you be so cruel?" the Marquis asked. "It would break the child's heart, and also . . . ."

He stopped because there was a step on the stairs.

A moment later Robin, wearing only his shirt and trousers, came into the kitchen.

He ran to Ila and held up his face.

"I am sorry if I am late," he said, "but I slept, and slept. I expect it was because I was very tired."

Ila bent down and kissed him and for a moment his arms were round her neck.

Then he said:

"But I am wide awake now, and very hungry!"

It was then he saw the Marquis.

"Uncle Osbert! You are here!"

"I have come for my breakfast," the Marquis said, "and it is a good thing you have woken up otherwise I should have eaten it all and left you nothing."

Robin laughed.

"Ila would not let you do that!"

"No, of course I would not," Ila agreed, "and there is plenty here for all of us!"

"Did you ride here on *Saracen*?" Robin asked.

"He is outside," the Marquis replied.

"I will go and talk to him when I have had my breakfast," Robin said.

Ila put a plate of eggs, sausage and bacon before them both.

She chose two fried eggs for herself.

The loaf of bread was freshly baked and the Marquis and Robin ate large slices, thick with butter.

Then Ila toasted some of it in front of the stove.

They ate these with the honey she had been given by the Beekeeper.

She told the Marquis how kind he had been and said to Robin:

"We must go and thank him for it."

"I would like to see the hives," Robin said. "Papa tried to keep bees, but the mice got into the hives and ate all the honey."

"That was certainly a disaster!' the Marquis exclaimed. "But I expect if it had not been the mice, it would have been a little boy called 'Robin' who gobbled it all up!"

He was laughing and teasing Robin.

Quite suddenly it struck Ila how strange it was that the Marquis of whom she had been so afraid should seem so at home in this tiny kitchen.

The three of them might have been an ordinary village family enjoying the first meal of the day.

"He is very, very different," she told herself again, "from what I . . expected him . . to be like!"

Then she was afraid of her own thoughts.

As soon as they had finished, Robin wanted to go out to see *Saracen*.

When Ila came back from the scullery he had gone.

"Will he be all right?" she asked the Marquis.

"He will come to no harm with *Saracen*," the Marquis answered, "and I think it is good for him to be independent."

He had shut the door.

As Ila walked to the window to make sure Robin was quite safe, he said quietly:

"What are you going to do about him, Ila? I am quite certain that if you go away again he will follow you."

She did not move from the window. But she knew he was speaking the truth.

Silently she was asking herself:

"What . . am I to . . do?"

She had a feeling she was speaking to her mother, just as she had told Robin to speak to his.

She did not hear the Marquis rise and come to stand just behind her.

"Robin loves you," he said very quietly, "and so, Ila, do I!"

She was very still.

She thought that what she had heard must be a figment of her imagination.

Then in a voice that did not sound like her own, she asked:

"W.what are you . . saying? I . . I do not . . understand."

"I do not understand it myself," the Marquis replied. "But ever since I first saw you unconscious, you have haunted me."

There was a note in his voice which made Ila quiver.

Her face was still turned away from him.

"You are so beautiful," the Marquis said, "and at the same time so totally unlike anyone I have ever seen before that I do not believe you are real."

He laughed mockingly before he went on:

"I told myself it was because I was upset at what had happened to Robin, and it was all an illusion."

He drew a deep breath before saying:

"But I could think of nothing but you. Then when you opened the door last night, I knew that I was in love as I have never in my whole life, been in love before!"

It . . it is not . . possible!" Ila said in a voice that seemed to come from a very long distance away.

"If it is not love," the Marquis said, "then what is it that makes me want to take the stars and the moon from the sky and lay them at your feet?"

She felt him come a little nearer as he continued:

"I want to carry you into the heart of the sun – take you to the places in the world you described so vividly to Robin!"

Ila made a little murmur of surprise as the Marquis said:

"You drew him a picture of the Pyramids. I will take you there and we will see them by moonlight, and try to discover the secret which enabled the Egyptians to build anything so spiritual."

Ila turned to look at him as he went on:

"I will show you the Mosques in Turkey, and we will climb the Himalayas."

He drew in a deep breath as he added:

"I shall only be afraid that the gods who dwell on the unexplored peaks might claim you as their own, and I would lose you."

"H.how . . can you say such . . things to me?" Ila asked in a whisper.

"I am saying what I know you will understand as no one else would."

"That . . is what I . ." Ila said, then stopped.

"That is what you feel," the Marquis finished. "Do you not understand, my darling, what has happened? It is what I always believed was impossible – we fell in love with each other at first sight!"

Ila gave a little gasp.

"Is that . . really true?"

"I will prove it," the Marquis answered.

He put his arms around her very gently.

"Are you real?" he asked. "Or am I dreaming?"

Then his lips were on hers.

For a moment Ila felt too bemused, too bewildered to realise what was happening.

Then as he kissed her she felt the sunlight streaking through her body.

It was a rapture she had never know existed.

It was the beauty of the woods, the song of the birds, the scent of the flowers only more.

So much more it could only be expressed in music.

As the Marquis kissed her, and went on kissing her, she felt as if he really had carried her up, as he had said, to the sun.

They were enveloped in the glory of it.

This was love, the love she wanted: an ecstasy beyond words, beyond thought.

She knew as he drew her closer and still closer that they were no longer two people but one.

They were united by a love that was irresistible and inexplicable.

What she felt was so intense that it was almost a pain.

Yet it was a wonder, and a dazzling light.

She made a little murmur, and hid her head against his neck.

"My darling, my sweet, I have found you!" the Marquis said, and his voice was unsteady. "You are mine, and I will never lose you, never let you go!"

As if he were afraid this might happen, he turned her face up to his.

Then he was kissing her again, kissing her demandingly, fiercely, possessively.

She was not afraid, she only knew it was the most glorious thing that could happen.

The Marquis was the man of her dreams; the man who had ridden beside her in the wood and who believed in all the things she did.

He understood, as nobody else had ever been able to do.

When the Marquis raised his head again, she said a little incoherently'

"I . . I . . love you . . I . . love you!"

"As I love you, my precious little nymph," he replied. "How soon will you marry me?"

For a moment Ila was still.

Then she realised what was happening.

It was the Marquis of Rakemoore who was kissing her!

A man from whom she had run away and who had no idea who she really was.

She would have hidden her face once again against his neck, but he prevented her from doing so.

"Why are you worried?" he asked.

"How . . how do you . . know I am . . worried?"

"I know everything about you – everything you think, everything you dream. You are a part of me. Ila, as I am a part of you."

"Then . . you know I have . . something to . . tell you."

"The secret of why you have run away?" the Marquis asked. "It is of no importance because now there is no reason for you to be frightened any longer."

"But . . I am frightened!"

"Why?"

"Because . . you may be angry . . and not . . love me . . any more."

The Marquis laughed and it was a very happy sound.

"That is impossible! Now tell me why you are hiding, and from whom."

There was silence.

Then Ila said in a voice that trembled.

"From y.you!"

The Marquis stared at her.

"Me? I do not understand!"

"I . . I am . . Lavinia . . Worth."

For a second it seemed as if the Marquis had turned to stone.

"Please . . do not be . . angry," she pleaded. "Papa told me I had to . . m.marry a man I had never even seen! My sisters are so . . miserable in their marriages . . I thought I would rather . . d.die."

"So you ran away from me," the Marquis said.

"I ran away from the Marquis of Rakemoore, whom I thought was a . . pompous . . insensitive and . . arrogant man who would . . never understand what I felt . . about the w.woods!"

"I am beginning to understand," the Marquis said.

"B.but . . you are so very . . very different from what I . . expected."

"And so are you," the Marquis answered. "I thought you would be a dull, gauche, tiresome debutante."

He gave a short laugh.

"How could I have imagined for one moment that you were the Duke's daughter when to me you are the Spirit of the Woods, the dream that has been locked within my heart ever since I was a little boy and my mother died."

"Oh . . darling . . did you . . miss her as Robin . . misses his mother?" Ila asked.

"I missed her unbearably," the Marquis admitted. "But I had no Ila to explain to me that she was not dead, but looking after me, loving me, and very near me when I needed her."

"You . . know I said that to . . Robin?"

"I was listening at the door," the Marquis confessed. "It was then I knew it would be impossible for me to go on living without you."

"You . . do understand why I . . ran away?"

"Of course I understand. It is exactly what you should have done - from every man except me!"

"Oh . . I love you!" Ila cried.

There was no need for words, the Marquis kissed her again: kissed her until they were both breathless.

The small cottage seemed to be spinning dizzily around them.

He drew her across the kitchen to the small Parlour so that they could sit down on the sofa side by side.

"We have to make plans, my beautiful one," he said, "but it is difficult for me to think of anything except that I want to go on kissing you."

Ila gave a little sigh.

"I . . I suppose I must . . go home and tell . . Papa that I have . . changed my mind."

"Your father told me most convincingly first that you were visiting a sick relative, then that you had a bad cold and a temperature!"

Ila laughed a little guiltily.

"Poor Papa! He is so tremendously thrilled at the idea of having you for a son-in-law, you would think it was he who was marrying you rather than me!"

"I am sure he will forgive you for running away," the Marquis said, "especially when he knows there is now no opposition."

Ila put her head against the Marquis's shoulder.

"I thought just now . . when we were having breakfast," she said, "that we were like an ordinary village couple . . and it is . . wonderful having you to myself . . in this dear little cottage!"

"I am going to have you to myself in a great number of places," the Marquis said. "All I want, Ila, is to have you alone."

Ila sighed again.

"We will have to listen to all those people saying what a 'suitable' marriage it is, and somehow . . because they will talk and talk . . it will . . spoil the dream we are . . living in at the moment."

The Marquis' arms tightened round her.

"That is what I feel," he said, "and I have an answer to that problem, although you may not approve."

"All I want . . is to make . . you happy," Ila said softly. "How can you be so . . wonderful?"

The Marquis laughed.

"I have a feeling you were critical of me, not only because your father wanted you to marry me, but also for the way I treated Robin."

Ila did not answer, and he said:

"But I promise you it is something that will never happen again. You have shown me what was wrong, and I shall not make the same mistake with my own children because you will be there to guide me."

"I love you for being so understanding," Ila said, "and you could not have known, if no one told you, how much he missed his mother."

She stiffened before she said:

"Suppose he is . . upset at my . . marrying you? He might . . in some way feel . . jealous!"

"Leave that to me," the Marquis said, "and because I now have you I know what to do, my darling."

He touched her forehead softly with his lips before he said:

"You have not yet heard my solution to the problem of our wedding!"

Ila looked up at him and he said:

"What I would like to do would be to make you mine before we have to 'face the music'."

"How . . how can we do that?" Ila asked a little nervously.

"As you know, this village is part of my estate," the Marquis explained, "the living of the Church is mine, and I appoint the Vicar."

Ila looked puzzled and the Marquis went on:

"He is a kind man, and I know he will marry us immediately if I ask him to do so. If there are a few legal difficulties afterwards, the Archbishop of Canterbury is one of my Godfathers."

As he finished speaking, he remembered that the Queen was his Godmother.

He thought of the trap he had managed to avoid.

It seemed hardly possible that inadvertently through her he had found a perfect wife.

The woman who would fill the place in his life he had kept sacred.

They were found by the Divine love which all men seek, but few are privileged to find.

"Do you mean . . ." Ila was asking, "that we can be . . married . . without anyone else . . being there?"

"Nobody except Robin," the Marquis replied, "but of course, you must ask the angels, the nymphs from the pool and the spirits of the wood!"

Ila wanted to laugh with sheer happiness.

But it was impossible because he was kissing her.

It was a little later that the Marquis called Robin back into the cottage.

He came running immediately and when he entered the kitchen the Marquis said:

"I want to talk to you, Robin, and I suggest we go into the Parlour."

He had arranged this with Ila.

He left the door just ajar so that she could hear what was said.

The Marquis sat down in an armchair and Robin sat on the sofa.

"I want your help," the Marquis began.

"My help?" Robin exclaimed in surprise.

"It is about Ila. I am very afraid that you and I might lose her."

Robin gave a little cry.

"She is not thinking of running away again, Uncle Osbert? We must stop her!"

"That is what I want to do," the Marquis said, "but you will have to help me, and it is not very easy."

"What can I do?" Robin asked. "I cannot lose her! I love her, Uncle Osbert, and I want her to stay with me."

"I want her too," the Marquis answered, "and I have a plan of how we can do that, if we do it together."

Robin bent forward with his elbows on his knees and said:

"Tell me."

"I have thought it over," the Marquis said in a serious voice, "and the only way we can keep her with us for ever and ever is if I marry her!"

Robin stared at his Uncle.

"Do you mean – she would be your wife?"

"She would be my wife," the Marquis said, "and she would live with us at Rake, and in all my other houses."

Robin thought this over.

"Then she would not have to hide from the people who are trying to make her do what she did not want to do."

"Exactly! I knew you would understand," the Marquis said, "and because we do not want her to be upset so that she wants to run away I have suggested that I marry her at once, here in the village Church, and no one will know anything about it except you!"

"You mean – you are not inviting any of your friends?" Robin asked.

"There will be nobody but you to watch us being married," the Marquis said, "and you will have to be my Best Man, and hold the ring for me."

Robin's eyes were shining, and the Marquis went on:

"I will arrange for it to take place this afternoon. But no one must have the slightest idea what is happening. You must not mention it to anyone until Ila is my wife. After that she will never be frightened again."

Robin clapped his hands.

"That is a spiffing idea, Uncle Osbert, and of course I want to help you."

"Thank you very much, Robin, and when the wedding has taken place, Ila will belong to me and you for ever!"

Robin got to his feet and to the Marquis' surprise, flung his arms around his neck.

He kissed his Uncle on the cheek and the Marquis hugged him.

He told himself as he did so that he would want his sons to be like Robin, and to have his courage.

As the small boy moved away from him he got to his feet.

"I have quite a lot to do," he said, "so I am leaving Ila in your charge. You must not allow anybody to frighten her."

"I will do that, Uncle Osbert," Robin said proudly.

They went into the kitchen.

There was no need for Ila to tell the Marquis how clever he had been.

There were tears in her eyes as she smiled at him.

Waiting in the Church of St Mary's, the Marquis thought he had never done so many things so quickly.

He had ridden from the cottage to the Vicarage.

There he told the Vicar what he required.

He impressed on him that it was extremely important that his marriage should be kept a secret. Gratified at having such an important ceremony to perform, the Vicar agreed to everything he suggested.

As soon as the Marquis had left he hurried to find flowers for the Church from his own garden.

The Marquis had gone on to The House in the Wood.

When he told Nanny he intended to marry Ila she said:

"I knew as soon as I set eyes on her that she was exactly the sort of wife you should have, and the Good Lord has heard my prayers!"

"What I am asking you to do, Nanny," the Marquis said, "is to have Robin with you while we are on our honeymoon."

He paused to smile at her before he continued:

"I will send a groom over every day with his pony, so that he can ride. And I am sure Wilcox will find plenty to keep him occupied until we return."

"He'll be all right with me, Master Osbert, don't you worry about it!" Nanny said. "And I know Miss Ila will be a real mother to him, which is what he wants."

"She is what he wants, and what I want too," the Marquis said.

He told Nanny to keep their secret until tomorrow.

Then he spoke to Wilcox and they arranged something which he knew would delight Robin.

At Rake he gave a number of orders which Mr Barrett found somewhat bewildering.

He was too well trained to ask the Marquis any questions.

As the Marquis ate a quick luncheon on a tray he wrote a letter to the Duke.

He gave it to Mr Barrett and told him it was to be delivered tomorrow afternoon.

Not a minute earlier!

He thought it would not hurt the Duke to continue searching a little longer for his daughter.

When he learnt they were already on their honeymoon it might be a shock.

At the same time His Grace would have the son-in-law he wanted!

The Marquis told the Duke to go ahead with mating the mares with his stallion.

'That will keep him happy,' he thought with a twinkle in his eyes.

He then ordered a groom to ride to his home in the New Forest.

He said they would stay there for a few days.

His yacht was to come to the nearest harbour and be ready to go to sea.

His Head Chef from Rake was to go with him.

The Marquis ordered a closed carriage and changed his clothes.

Then he drove to Fording-Field.

He was dropped off at the Church.

The carriage went on to pick up Ila and a very excited Robin.

The Marquis had given the footman on the box an envelope for Robin.

When he opened it he found it contained a wedding ring.

It had belonged to the Marquis' mother.

He himself had in his pocket her engagement ring which he had always vowed to give to his wife, if he loved her.

Ila knew that nothing mattered except their love.

Nevertheless she wanted to look pretty on her wedding day.

She had brought with her one gown which was fortunately white.

It was made of a soft, light material which, like the green gown, made her look sylph-like and ethereal.

There was no lace veil as she would have worn if she had a grand wedding.

Instead she and Robin had picked flowers from the garden.

There were white pansies, white violets and a few lilies-of-the-valley.

Robin had also gone into the fields beyond the village to find magenta and cuckoo-flowers.

It was one of her Governesses who had taught her how to make daisy-chains, wreaths and posies.

They had collected wild flowers from the field round the castle.

Ila fashioned a wreath with all the white flowers. It was more becoming on her red-gold hair than any diamond tiara could have been.

She made herself a very pretty bouquet of all the long-stemmed flowers of every colour.

Because the Marquis did not want anyone at Rake to know what was happening, he brought no flowers back with him.

He thought, however, when he saw Ila coming up the aisle hand-in-hand with Robin that she might have come from the field of Olympus.

She was even more beautiful than he remembered her to be.

There was no one in the Church but the Vicar.

Someone unseen was playing very softly on the organ.

When Ila reached the Marquis she put out her hand.

His fingers closed over hers.

She felt then that their vibrations joined.

They were so close already that even the Marriage Service could not make them any closer.

She had told Robin exactly what he had to do.

He gave her away, then moved to the side of the Marquis.

He was waiting to hand him the wedding ring when he asked for it.

As the Marquis slipped it onto Ila's finger he thanked God that by a miracle he was marrying a woman he loved.

He knew Ila loved him just for himself and not for who he was or what he possessed.

They drove away from the Church.

Not even the most 'nosey' person in the village had the slightest idea what had taken place.

Robin was sitting on the seat opposite them and when Rake was in sight, the Marquis said:

167

"You will understand, Robin, that Ila and I want to be alone tonight, and tomorrow we are going away on our honeymoon."

He saw Robin's face fall, and he said quickly:

"I want you to go to Nanny's while we are away, and I have arranged for you to have anything you want while you are there."

He smiled at the boy before he continued:

"Wilcox wants you to help him, and *Firefly* will be brought over every day for you to exercise him. Also my Curator will be bringing you all the books you require from the Library, and others he will buy you."

He saw that Robin was listening and he went on:

"Ila and I will write to you from every place we go so that you will be able to look them up on maps and know exactly where we are, and we will also send pictures."

Robin was looking a little forlorn, and the Marquis said cheerfully:

"Another time, we will take you with us, but you must forgive me, Robin, if I am selfish in having Ila alone on our honeymoon."

"I understand," Robin said a little reluctantly.

"Wilcox tells me," the Marquis went on, "that one of my hunting spaniels has six puppies. He is going to choose one for himself and I thought you would like one!"

"A puppy for me?" Robin cried.

"You can train it while you are with Nanny."

"I would like that," Robin said. "Can it sleep with me?"

"Of course," the Marquis agreed, "and you must feed it and it must be with you all the time until it knows you are its master."

"I will make him very good and obedient," Robin said looking at Ila.

"I know you will," she said, "and you will tell him to look after you and protect you until we return."

She held out her arms as she spoke.

As the carriage came to standstill she held him very close and they kissed each other.

As they stepped out of the carriage a groom was coming round the building with *Firefly*.

Ila watched as the Marquis kissed Robin then lifted him into the saddle.

"I would like you to come up to the stables occasionally,' the Marquis told him, "to see that the horses are all right.'

"I will do that," Robin promised.

"And get Nanny to tell you some of the tales she used to tell me when I was about your age," the Marquis added. "She knows lots and lots of stories which I think you will find exciting."

Ila squeezed Robin's hand.

"We will not be away for long,' she said, "and I promise we will send you letters and postcards from all the places we go to."

Robin bent down and kissed her again.

"I shall be thinking of you all the time you are away," he said.

He rode off and Ila waved until he was out of sight.

Then she and the Marquis walked into the hall.

"I want you to congratulate me, Dawson," the Marquis said to the Butler. "Lady Lavinia and I have just been married, and you are the first to know about it!"

Dawson rose to the occasion.

"That's very good news, M'Lord – very good news indeed, and I wish you and Her Ladyship every happiness!"

"Thank you," the Marquis replied.

"Mr Barrett has ordered some champagne to be ready for you, My Lord, in the Study."

"We will have it later," the Marquis said. "I want first

to show Her Ladyship the room she will be using, which was my mother's."

The Marquis took Ila up the stairs.

Looking round her, she thought that Rake was the most impressive house she had ever imagined.

It was something, she thought, which might have come out of her dreams.

The bedroom into which the Marquis took her was very beautiful.

There were flowers everywhere, orchids, lilies, and a profusion of other blossoms which scented the air.

She looked around her.

Then as the Marquis closed the door behind him she turned towards him.

"I am dreaming . . I know I am dreaming!" she said. "Please, darling, kiss me . . in case I wake up!"

The Marquis laughed.

Then he put his arms around her.

He kissed her until they were both floating in the sky.

Ila knew there were stars in her breast, and the sun was enveloping them with a light which came from God.

"You are mine!" the Marquis said. "Mine, and no one shall ever take you from me!"

"How could they?" Ila asked. "I am yours . . completely and . . absolutely yours!"

Very gently he took the wreath from her hands.

He pulled out the pins until her hair fell over her shoulders.

"This is how I wanted to see you, Heart of my Heart, my nymph, my soul," he said hoarsely.

Then there was only the music of the wood, the scent of the flowers, and Love which had joined them together for all Eternity.

Barbara Cartland
The Temple of Love £1.99

When they came to the stone carving of the King, Sarida pulled back the vines so that the Duke could see his own face. . . .

To avoid an importunate mistress, the Duke of Inglebury undertakes a special assignment for the Viceroy of India and travels incognito into the heart of Java in search of an ancient Buddhist temple.

There he encounters its self-appointed guardian, Sarida, a lovely English girl caring for her invalid father. She shares the Duke's astonishment at finding he bears an uncanny resemblance to the sculpture of a Hindu King with herself in the likeness of his Princess.

Time is precious, for the treasures of the Temple are threatened by thieves and Sarida's virtue is under siege from the licentious Dutch colonel of the local garrison. There are many dangers to be overcome before Sarida and the Duke can share a love that came from eternity and would go on to eternity.

Barbara Cartland
A Revolution of Love £1.99

"Help! Help me . . . please . . . help me!" Drogo looked up in astonishment and saw the figure of a woman. She was hanging from a rope down a high wall beside which he was walking. . . .

Hotly pursued by Russian agents, Drogo Forde escapes from Afghanistan into neighbouring Kozan after completing a highly secret mission. Even then safety eludes him as revolutionaries storm the royal palace in an orgy of violence.

Now Drogo faces two problems. How to safeguard his vital information, and, equally important, how to protect the lovely Thekla who entered his life in such a very unconventional manner – before revealing her true identity.

An old cargo boat seemingly offers the only safety, the price a marriage of convenience that swiftly blossoms into the rapture of a shared love. The days and nights are bitter sweet for danger lurks at their journey's end, and heartbreak too, for how could a commoner be allowed to marry a Princess of Royal blood?

Barbara Cartland
A Hazard of Hearts £2.99

Serena looked at the Marquis of Vulcan in astonishment and was suddenly aware her knees felt very weak.
'Are you afraid of love, or merely of – me?'
'Of both,' Serena replied. . .

Her freedom lost on the turn of a card, Serena is bound by a debt of honour to marry Justin Marquis of Vulcan, a heartless cynic and the most handsome man she had ever seen.

Accompanying Justin to Mandrake, his ancestral home, Serena enters a house of evil ruled by his mother, the imperious Marchioness of Vulcan, and encounters a hatred such as she had never known.

Learning by chance the dark secrets of this strange family. Serena becomes trapped in a world of smugglers, highwaymen, gilded salons, subterranean passages, abduction and – murder!

There was much to hate at Mandrake yet the outcome of a duel sends Serena on a headlong gallop through the gathering darkness. Would her ride to Justin be like her love – in vain?

Barbara Cartland
The Passionate Princess £2.50

"Now we have found each other, you fill the whole world."

With a stab of fear Thea realised that the men who came from behind the trees and encircled them were bandits.

Thea never thought that her flight from the Royal Palace would end like this – a prisoner of the very men who spread terror throughout the Balkans, and saved from shame and humiliation by the courage of Nikos.

It was only yesterday she had met the tall, broad-shouldered artist and sheltered in his little house on the mountainside. Only this afternoon that the magic of the gypsy violins echoed what was in their hearts.

Now as the solitary torch in their cave flickered and died, Thea heard Nikos propose marriage. Could she renounce her birthright? Was she to be denied the love she craved because she was a Royal Princess?

All these books are available at your local bookshop or newsagent, or can be ordered direct from the publisher. Indicate the number of copies required and fill in the form below.

Send to: **CS Department, Pan Books Ltd., P.O. Box 40, Basingstoke, Hants.   RG21 2YT.**

or phone: 0256 469551 (Ansaphone), quoting title, author and Credit Card number.

Please enclose a remittance* to the value of the cover price plus: 60p for the first book plus 30p per copy for each additional book ordered to a maximum charge of £2.40 to cover postage and packing.

*Payment may be made in sterling by UK personal cheque, postal order, sterling draft or international money order, made payable to Pan Books Ltd.

Alternatively by Barclaycard/Access:

Card No.

Signature:

Applicable only in the UK and Republic of Ireland.

While every effort is made to keep prices low, it is sometimes necessary to increase prices at short notice. Pan Books reserve the right to show on covers and charge new retail prices which may differ from those advertised in the text or elsewhere.

NAME AND ADDRESS IN BLOCK LETTERS PLEASE:

....

Name ————————————————————————————————

Address ————————————————————————————————

————————————————————————————————

————————————————————————————————

————————————————————————————————

3/87